Someone had breached the premises.

"Mason, wake up. We need to get out of here. They found us!"

He stirred and blinked open his eyes.

Emma leaned closer to whisper. "Mason, can you hear me?"

"Em? What happened?"

"Someone rammed their vehicle into the house." She glanced toward the obliterated wall.

A shadow passed in front of the glowing headlights.

"We need to get out of here. Now!"

Mason eased himself up and pointed. "Gun. Flashlight. Cell phone. Laptop. Nightstand." His raspy words divulged his condition.

Would a possible concussion inhibit their escape? She ignored the question and grabbed his belongings.

"I'll take Sierra. You know how to shoot, right?"

"Yes." She stuffed his laptop in the backpack and his cell phone in her pocket.

Mason lifted her daughter into his arms. "We'll go out the back. You cover us."

Emma squashed the overwhelming sensation of dread. She couldn't stop now. Their lives depended on their escape...

Darlene L. Turner is an award-winning author who lives with her husband, Jeff, in Ontario, Canada. Her love of suspense began when she read her first Nancy Drew book. She's turned that passion into her writing and believes readers will be captured by her plots, inspired by her strong characters and moved by her inspirational message. Visit Darlene at www.darlenelturner.com, where there's suspense beyond borders.

Books by Darlene L. Turner

Love Inspired Suspense

Border Breach
Abducted in Alaska
Lethal Cover-Up
Safe House Exposed

Visit the Author Profile page at LoveInspired.com.

SAFE HOUSE EXPOSED

DARLENE L. TURNER

LOVE INSPIRED SUSPENSE
INSPIRATIONAL ROMANCE

LOVE INSPIRED® SUSPENSE

INSPIRATIONAL ROMANCE

ISBN-13: 978-1-335-72297-3

Recycling programs for this product may not exist in your area.

Safe House Exposed

Copyright © 2022 by Darlene L. Turner

This edition published by arrangement with Harlequin Books S.A.

For questions and comments about the quality of this book, please contact us at CustomerService@Harlequin.com.

Love Inspired
22 Adelaide St. West, 41st Floor
Toronto, Ontario M5H 4E3, Canada
www.LoveInspired.com

Printed in U.S.A.

For I know the thoughts that I think toward you, saith the Lord, thoughts of peace, and not of evil, to give you an expected end.
—*Jeremiah* 29:11

For Mom and Dad.

I miss you.

Acknowledgments

Jeff, thank you for your continued support and encouragement in my writing journey. Love you!

To Susan and Natalie, my beautiful sisters. I appreciate you cheering me on even when discouragement rears its ugly head. Mom and Dad T, I'm grateful for you both.

Suspense Squad sisters, thank you for all the brainstorming and advice. You're the best!

Darlene's Border Patrol, you're amazing. Thank you!

Brenda, Diane, Priscilla, Louise and Sandra—thank you for reading my books before I press Send. Love you.

Lisa, Stephanie, Heather, Rita, Barbara and Ruth, we spent many hours learning the writing craft. I appreciate you.

DiAnn Mills, thank you for your mentorship. Go, redheads!

To Tina James, my editor, and Tamela Hancock Murray, my agent, thank you for your support and helping my stories come to life!

Jesus. May I always remember why I write. For You. Thank You for loving me...all the time.

ONE

Fork lightning flashed from one dark, haunting cloud to another, sending a shiver bolting throughout police constable Mason James's body. He shrugged off the aura of dread and pulled onto the Peace Bridge connecting Buffalo, New York, and Fort Erie, Ontario. The weather matched his foul mood after hitting another dead end in his investigation of a leak within the Canadian Witness Protection Program. Someone had sold witness locations, and Chief Superintendent Seth James had tasked Mason to go undercover to find the mole.

The sound of thunder booming as the rain pelted across his windshield almost drowned out the call coming through his Bluetooth. He glanced at the screen and grimaced.

His father, looking for answers.

Mason punched the button. "Hey, what's up?"

"Did you get any leads?"

Right to business. No hello. Nothing. *Just like you, Dad*. Mason imagined the day he'd live up to his father's expectations like Brady. His cop brother could never do wrong.

The thought of disappointing his father again stabbed at his tightened chest muscles. "Dead end."

"We need a break in this case, son. No mistakes on this one. Lives close to us are depending on you."

He didn't miss the forced tone in Chief Superintendent Seth James's voice. Mason needed to curb what he wanted to say, so he counted to five in his head before responding. "I know, Dad. My informant wasn't where he said he'd be. Not my fault."

"Listen, I was just notified of another witness in the program who's been targeted. It's—" He paused, his voice quivering.

Mason straightened in the driver's seat. "Who is it, Dad? I'm just—"

Crunch!

The rear-end collision sent his pickup lurching toward oncoming bridge traffic. The black SUV shot around him, wove in and out of the lanes and sped toward Canada's border. Mason tightened his grip and swerved right, but not in time to avoid the car in the opposite lane clipping his front end. They both careened toward the edge as another vehicle rammed him from behind.

Multiple cars smashed into each other. Mason's truck finally came to a stop next to the bridge's edge.

"Son, what's going on?" his father shouted.

Mason had forgotten the chief's call in the seconds of the crash. "Multicar pileup on the Peace Bridge. Dad, call in emergency response. I gotta go." He punched off the call and jumped out of his truck.

Another driver exited his car. "You okay? What happened?"

Good question. The SUV had purposely rammed Mason, and a thought dashed into his mind.

Someone had blown his cover. It was the only way they would've known he'd traveled to Buffalo to meet with an informant.

Mason shrugged. "Not exactly sure. Let's check the occupants of the other cars."

The man nodded.

After inspecting all the vehicles and passengers, he breathed a sigh of relief. No injuries.

Mason walked to the railing and peeked over the edge at the deadly Niagara River. This crash could have been much worse.

A flash of lightning filled the sky, followed seconds later by a crack of thunder as rain hammered the area. Being in the open in a thunderstorm on a bridge was not a good combination and could prove fatal. He gazed at the darkened clouds, willing them to dissipate.

Forty-five minutes later, after helping emergency response tend to the accident, Mason remembered his father's call. He turned to an officer. "I need to leave to assist in another situation. Stay safe."

He jumped back into his dented truck. Thankfully, the damage didn't affect his vehicle's drivability. He punched in his dad's number and wove around the scene. Mason hated to leave, but he had no choice.

"Everyone okay at the accident?" his father asked, his voice filled with concern.

"Dad, this was *not* an accident. A black SUV intentionally rammed me from behind and sped off before I got his license plate. I'm concerned my cover has been blown."

"How? Very few know of your involvement."

"Good question." Mason approached the E-ZPass border lane, which would allow him to cross back into Canada without difficulty. "What were you telling me earlier? What witness is compromised?"

A heavy exhale swept through the Bluetooth. "Emma. Sierra is with her."

"What? How?" Mason's grip on the wheel tightened. His sister-in-law was a Canada Border Services Agency officer, and her four-year-old daughter was the apple of his father's eye.

No wonder the rough and tough veteran officer's guard had weakened after receiving the news. He doted on the little girl. Guilt pricked Mason's conscience. He couldn't remember the last time he'd visited Emma and Sierra. His father had requested he stay away. The man's agenda had been clear— they didn't need a reminder of Brady. Mason fought his father, stating he wanted to help the girls, but ultimately he'd lost the battle.

"Mason, don't you listen to the news?"

He suppressed the groan he wanted to expel. Once again, Chief Superintendent James expected his son to be the police force's best officer. A pressure Mason would prefer to do without. "Dad, I've been a tad busy in my deep-cover assignment with not much contact with the outside world. What is it?"

"Her joint task force uncovered a smuggling ring and tied it back to Lincoln Luther with solid evidence."

What? The Buffalo Luther crime family was notorious, and anyone who got in their way… well, Mason refused to speculate what the son and daughter of this family would do to those who messed with the Luthers, especially their father.

"Why wasn't I told she was in the program?"

Silence.

You didn't want me in her life just like before, did you? Mason took the next turn sharply. "Never mind. What do you need me to do?"

"Head to her safe house. Protect her." A pause. "At *all* costs." His father rattled off the address.

Mason didn't miss his emphasis on the word *all*. The question was—

Would Emma accept his help after the way he'd treated her since the accident that took his brother Brady's life three years ago?

He brushed off his guilt and stepped on the accelerator. "On it."

"Be careful, son." His dad ended the call.

Mason pulled into the undisclosed home's driveway off the beaten path near Fort Erie ten minutes later. His father had not placed her far enough away. Why? He banged the steering wheel before putting the truck into Park. The thought of facing Emma James caused his shoulder muscles to bunch up. He rubbed them and inhaled, remembering the promise he'd made to Brady at his grave site.

I will always look after your family.

Mason's failure to help his sister-in-law and niece gnawed at him like a beaver chewing on a tree trunk. He had broken his oath to his brother. He rolled his shoulders back and turned off the engine. Time to work on fulfilling his promise.

He jumped from the truck, hurried up the front steps and knocked.

Constable Darlene Seymour opened the door a crack, eyes widening. "Mason. I thought you were out of the country."

A cover his father had fabricated.

Not even Mason's partner, Darlene, knew the truth. They had to plug the leak, and his dad had warned him to trust no one.

Darlene allowed him to enter.

"I'm back." He wouldn't blow the mission even if it had been compromised. "I need to see the witness."

A gasp sounded behind the constable.

Emma James stepped into the open. "Mason?" Her eyes narrowed.

Guilt once again prickled the back of his neck, the urge to flee increasing.

But his promise to Brady held Mason in his tracks.

He would not disappoint his brother again.

Canadian border patrol officer Emma James tensed at the sight of her brother-in-law. *You ignored us for the past few years, so why are you here now?* His sporadic presence after the tragic accident that had killed her husband, Brady, had told her one thing—Mason was avoiding her. Why, she didn't know.

Emma blamed herself for her husband's death. If she and Brady hadn't gotten into a fight on that stormy winter night, he wouldn't have rushed out of the house. Guilt over his death had haunted her for three long years, even though it meant she didn't have to live with any more of his abusive ways. A secret she'd kept from everyone, especially his family.

Her focus needed to be on her daughter, Sierra. Her pride and joy.

And the only reminder of her malicious husband.

Well, that and the man standing in the foyer. His resemblance to Brady punched her in the gut. A wave of nausea rose, and she swallowed to suppress it. She must put the past behind her to keep Sierra safe.

Emma clasped her hands in a vise grip. "What's going on, Mason?"

He gestured her into the living room and turned to Constable Seymour. "Darlene, can you give us a minute?"

The woman nodded and walked down the hall, her department-issued boots clunking on the hardwood.

Emma sat on the worn sofa and stared at the wall, ignoring his gaze. "Where have you been?" Her tone held animosity, but she knew she needed to rein it in. She'd gotten her and Sierra's lives to a new version of normalcy after Brady's death.

Until now.

Unless the threat against her ended, she would never see her friends and family again. She'd voluntarily entered herself and Sierra into the Canadian Witness Protection Program to stay under the Luther family's radar. It hadn't been what she wanted, but Emma had no choice.

Sierra's life depended on the protection. She would not lose her daughter. She expelled a heavy sigh and glanced back at Mason.

He walked over to the window and parted the blinds.

Probably checking on the constable seated in an unmarked vehicle down the street. Her father-in-law had seen to her protection.

Mason left his perch and plunked himself in the chair opposite her. "How are you, Emma?"

"Been better."

"Sierra?"

She smiled. The only light in her life at the moment had sung a song to her mama before she nestled into the bed for her afternoon nap. "She's good. Asleep right now."

"Time to get her up. We need to move you."

Emma's muscles tightened. "What? Again? Why?"

"Dad feels your location has been compromised."

"Already? We just got here." She bit her lip. "Surely the Luther family doesn't know where I am."

"We can't risk it."

"You didn't answer my earlier question. Where have you been? Why haven't you visited your niece?" Questions she had wanted explained for the past few years.

His hazel eyes clouded.

She'd hit a nerve.

"I'm sorry, but it couldn't be helped. Dad sent me deep undercover." Mason averted his gaze.

He wasn't telling her everything. Did he forget she was excellent at reading body language—a skill of a border patrol officer? "Please be honest with me."

Mason exhaled. "Someone within WPP or WIT-SEC is selling witness locations. We've lost some in both Ontario and New York, so Dad sent me underground to flush out the mole."

"And?"

"Still nothing. I've had leads, but none have panned out yet. And now I believe my cover was blown. We can't risk that they know your location."

"So, you're not entirely sure?" She didn't dare leave the safe house. The more they moved, the more exposed they'd be. Sierra had already been through enough.

"Dad received a tip and sent me to relocate you. He no longer trusts anyone else." He tapped his finger on his leg. "How did you get involved with the Luthers in the first place?"

"Long story. The short of it is, my superintendent put me on a task force with my US counterparts in Buffalo after we caught tourists trying to smuggle souvenirs from Niagara Falls loaded with drugs." She kneaded the knot in her neck.

"What type?"

"Heroin, fentanyl, ketamine. You name it."

"How did you tie the ring to Lincoln Luther?"

She twirled a strand of red hair around her finger. "That was the hard part. An informant snitched—Lincoln hired thugs to pose as tourists to go across the Fort Erie/Buffalo and the Niagara Falls borders. They'd drive to the falls on both sides and meet with members of his organization, buy the laced souvenirs and take them back across. Then sell the drugs on the street at an elevated price."

Mason whistled. "So the Luthers were making thousands."

"Millions."

"How long has this been going on?"

"At least two years. That we discovered." Emma stood, walked over to the fireplace and fingered an old clock sitting on the mantel. The loud ticking reminded her of the grandfather clock in her parents' home. The realization she would probably never see them again brought another wave of sadness. Her shoulders slumped. *God? What are You doing to me?* She believed in Jesus and had asked Him into her life as a child, but her husband's death, and now this circumstance, plagued her. She'd thought her life was perfectly planned out. Marriage. Child. Wonderful career.

Had God forgotten about her?

"Emma?"

She turned.

Mason had said something, and she'd missed his question.

No wonder, as she hadn't slept much in the past forty-eight hours. Exhaustion had set in and her body craved sleep, but the nightmare of losing Sierra tormented her, so she refused to lay her head on the pillow. She'd chosen to read instead of closing her eyes.

"Sorry, what did you say?" she asked.

"You okay?"

She rubbed the bridge of her nose. "Just tired."

"Please sit and continue." His expression softened.

Catching her off guard.

Brady's eyes stared back at her.

She ignored Mason's gaze and sank onto the sofa. Even though her husband had abused her, she'd still loved him and took his death hard. "After we figured out their process, we set up a sting and caught some so-called tourists. They ratted out Lincoln and his organization. Their testimony along with other evidence sealed his conviction. The tourists were all put into WPP and WITSEC."

"But why did you only enter after the trial was over?"

"I thought we were safe, as the trial went well. Almost too perfect." She fingered her rose-gold heart pendant. The one keepsake from her mother Seth had let her keep after her begging episode. "After the trial concluded, I started receiving threatening texts. Even a picture of Sierra playing at a park."

Mason's lips flattened as he clenched his fingers. "The Luthers discovered your identity. What about the rest of the task force?"

"Same. WPP and WITSEC." Once again, she twirled a strand of hair. "I volunteered to go into it. To protect Sierra. Even if it meant never seeing my family again."

A tear escaped.

She brushed it away.

He cleared his throat and stood. "We need to get you moved."

"To where?"

"Dad is working on securing another location. Somewhere farther away, I hope."

"Do we have to? You even said you weren't sure this place was exposed. Sierra likes it here."

"We just can't—"

The front window shattered.

Multiple Molotov cocktails smashed onto the hardwood floor. Flames erupted, clawing at anything in their path.

Emma bolted off the sofa. Mason was right.

She had been compromised.

TWO

Mason grabbed Emma's arm and rushed her down the hall as Darlene emerged from a room, gun in hand. He instructed his partner to call 911 and contact the other constable watching from the street. Mason turned to Emma. "Get Sierra. Leave everything behind. We can restock supplies. Bring nothing that can identify you."

Emma's eyes widened. "I need my glucose kit. I don't go anywhere without it."

Right. He'd forgotten about her diabetes. "That's fine. Nothing else." Smoke levels increased throughout the moderate-size home. "Get your daughter."

Emma nodded and raced into the middle bedroom. Moments later, she returned carrying a sleeping Sierra wrapped in a plaid blanket and clutching a stuffed giraffe. Emma had her medical bag flung over her shoulder.

"Leave the giraffe. We'll get a new one."

"What? No." She stepped closer to him. "When she wakes up and doesn't have Jerome, she'll go ballistic," she whispered.

Mason flinched. Her minty breath and vanilla scent permeated his personal space. That and her gorgeous emerald-green eyes played on his emotions.

Guilt tugged at his chest and pushed him backward. She was his sister-in-law, but he understood why his brother had said he got lost in her eyes. Over and over.

He shook off the memory and nodded. "Fine. We need to move."

Flames had now engulfed the living room and moved toward them at rapid speed. They had little time left until the entire house burned down.

Darlene scrambled through the back door. "Constable Fuller was shot. That's how they got by him. I don't see the assailants but suspect they're close. Emergency vehicles are en route."

Their escape seemed impossible.

Emma coughed.

They didn't have a choice but to move. He couldn't risk any further smoke inhalation. "Cover us, Darlene." He turned to Emma. "Stay behind me."

She nodded.

He raised his weapon and followed Darlene out the back door.

The female constable lifted her Smith & Wesson in all directions, checking for the suspects before handing him her keys. "I drove my undercover vehicle today to stay under the wire. Take it. Your truck doesn't look like you'd get far."

"What about Sierra?" Mason hadn't thought ahead about transporting his niece. He hadn't had time to think about much before his dad tasked him as Emma's protector.

"Got ya covered. Remember, I have a young son. Nice to have you back, partner." She pointed. "Go!" She ran around the house's corner.

Multiple shots boomed at her appearance.

Emma yelped.

Sierra woke up and screamed.

Darlene scrambled back and hid behind a massive oak tree to the left of the lane. She peeked out and fired.

Flames shot from the roof. The house was lost. A pungent, soot-infested smell assaulted Mason's nostrils. He had to get them out of here. *Lord, keep us safe.* Not that he and God were close right now, but his mother's steadfast faith had impressed him—even through every struggle in her life.

"Go!" Darlene yelled and fired again.

Mason crouch-walked over and opened the back door. "Get in and stay down with Sierra."

Sirens sounded in the near distance. Help for Darlene had arrived. *Thank You.* Now he didn't feel guilty leaving his partner alone with who knew how many suspects hiding nearby.

He jumped into the driver's seat and hit the engine start button. He glanced behind him to ensure Emma and Sierra were safely concealed. "Hang on."

Mason stepped on the gas and screeched from

the paved driveway, keeping his head lowered. He wasn't about to give the shooters an easy target.

A bullet hit the windshield.

His heart hammering in his chest, he peeked up and looked in the rearview mirror. A cruiser pulled up to the house, and constables scrambled out to help their fellow officer.

A black SUV fled in the opposite direction. Was it the same vehicle from the bridge? He'd contact Darlene to find out if they got the license plate.

Relief washed over him, and his shoulders relaxed. They were safe. For now. "You can put Sierra in the seat. The perps are gone."

Emma cleared her throat. "Did you catch a glimpse of them?"

"No time, but it looks like the same vehicle that tried to run me off the Peace Bridge."

"What? You didn't tell me that."

"Sorry, no time." Mason turned onto a side street. He'd take them from Fort Erie and contact his father for a new location.

"Do you think it's related to the Luthers?"

Mason stole a glance over his shoulder.

Emma moved Sierra into the child seat and fastened her in. Sierra whimpered. "Shh, baby girl. Mama's got you." She tickled the four-year-old's belly.

Sierra giggled. Fat tears still rolled down her

cheeks and intermixed with her red curls. "Mama. Tickle."

Mason returned his eyes to the road. The sight pushed his desire for a family back into his head. The recurring question niggled him.

How could he have a family and stay in this dangerous undercover position? No, he wouldn't put a wife and child through the angst his father had put Isabelle James through. His mother had shared her fears with Mason when he announced he wanted to become a cop like his father.

"Are you sure?" she had asked. "I worry every day your father is out on patrol. Are you going to do that to your wife?"

But he had told her then he would never marry.

She had only rolled her eyes at him.

"Earth to Mason. Do you think the two are related?"

Emma brought his focus back to the task at hand. Where it should be.

"If I doubted it earlier, I don't now." Mason drove farther until he came to a back alley he'd used when meeting with his informant Skip Perry. It was off the beaten path. He pulled in behind the older buildings.

"Why are we stopping?"

"I need to call my dad and get a new location." Mason fished out his cell phone and hit his father's number.

"Where are you?" Seth James's rough voice revealed his displeasure.

However, Mason knew the chief superintendent's anger hid his actual emotion. Fear for his granddaughter's life.

"In Skip's meeting place. Dad, we need a new location. Somewhere outside Fort Erie."

Keyboard clicks sailed through the phone. "Go to Thorold." He gave Mason the address of a home on the small city's outskirts. "I've dispatched a team to get it ready."

"Do you trust this team?"

His father exhaled. "I only trust you and Emma, but the members of this unit have been on my force for years. Set up other witnesses safely. Emma and my Tiddlywinks okay?"

Mason smiled at his father's term of endearment for his granddaughter. Cute.

He turned around to face Emma.

Her widened eyes told him they were anything but okay.

And Sierra? The same green eyes peered out at him from behind her stuffed giraffe.

"They're safe. For now." Mason repositioned himself and glanced out the front windshield. His heart lurched at the sight of both of them in the back seat.

He prayed he could keep his promise.

Forty-five minutes later, he pulled into the safe house's driveway near Thorold and parked. His cell phone buzzed in his pocket, and he took it out. His father. "I gotta take this. Stay here until I get back." He climbed from the vehicle and walked to a nearby tree. "Hey, Dad."

"Just checking in. How are my girls?"

"Fine. We just got here and are about to go inside the house."

"Are you two getting along? Son, it's time to step it up. Come back to the family."

Really, Dad? Mason had ignored family gatherings for the past few years, at his father's strange request. He had said Mason had reminded Emma too much of Brady, and Mason had reluctantly agreed to stay away.

Truth be told, guilt still plagued him over the last words he'd spoken to Brady. Mason clamped his eyes closed, shutting out his brother's accident scene. The transport truck had hit him head-on, and Brady had died instantly.

"We're fine, Dad. Any updates?" Mason needed to concentrate on the case.

"Just one. Constable Seymour caught the license plate number, and we got a hit."

"Who's it registered to?"

"Your informant, Skip Perry."

No way.

His informant had never betrayed Mason. A question entered his mind.

Had the Luthers' pocketbook been too great of a temptation for Skip?

* * *

Emma stared at the quaint ranch-style home. She prayed it was far away from the Luther family's clutches. However, from what she'd learned about the crime boss in the team's investigation, even the moon wasn't enough distance between them. The threat she had received remained forever etched in her mind.

WE'RE COMING AFTER YOU AND YOUR SWEET DAUGHTER, SIERRA. DON'T THINK WE WON'T FIND YOU WHEREVER YOU GO. WE HAVE EYES EVERYWHERE.

It didn't take her long to reach out to her father-in-law to check into the WPP. Yes, it meant disappearing from her parents' and sister's lives, but Sierra's life was at stake.

Emma would do anything for her sweet baby girl.

The small farm home in front of her was nestled between neighboring houses, but distanced enough that it would give her and Sierra privacy. She liked that.

Lord, help this place be safe. Sierra required stability, and changing locations did not help.

Mason opened the back door. "Shall we check it out?"

She nodded and turned to Sierra. "Want to see your new home, baby girl?"

"Yes, Mama!"

Fat raindrops plopped on the windshield, and Emma checked the late-summer sky. Once again the clouds had darkened, the earlier storm showing signs of returning with a vengeance.

Sierra hated storms.

"I've got her." Mason held out his arms. "Come to Uncle Mason, Sierra."

The little girl's eyes bulged, her lip quivering before she screamed.

Of course she'd react that way. She didn't do well with strangers.

And her uncle was definitely a stranger.

Emma rubbed Sierra's arm consolingly. "It's okay. Uncle Mason won't hurt you."

Mason grabbed Jerome and wiggled the toy in front of the girl's face. "Jerome wants to say hi. He needs a hug." He played a game to entice her out of her state.

She stopped crying, grabbed her giraffe, hugged it and sang a four-year-old's version of "You Are My Sunshine."

Emma chuckled. "Wow. She never comes out of one of her states that easily. You must have a special touch."

"Does she have these often?"

"Ever since Brady died." Emma tousled her daughter's red locks. "I think she misses her dad, even though she was only one at the time of his death." She paused. "Although your father has stepped in to help bridge the loss. He spoils her."

"I bet he does. How are you doing with everything?"

She pursed her lips. "I'm fine. Took you this long to ask?"

He tilted his head, a Brady quirk telling her he didn't understand.

She ignored his unspoken question and unbuckled her daughter. "Time to go, Sierra."

Mason lifted the child out and placed the blanket over her head and pulled it back off again. "Wanna play peekaboo?"

Sierra nodded.

Interesting. Her daughter rarely warmed up quickly to someone new. Did Sierra have a memory of Brady since the men looked so much alike?

Emma ignored the question and opened her door. Time to get in from the pending storm and to safety. She hoped.

The trio walked up the farm steps and across the veranda. The front door opened before they could knock. A man hurried toward them.

Emma jumped.

The thirtysomething man raised his hands. "It's okay. I'm Constable Tom Lucas, and I recently joined the chief's setup team. I'm tasked to secure your new home."

Something prickled the back of her neck, telling her they weren't alone.

Emma froze in place. Stealing a glance over her shoulder, she scanned the area, her law enforcement skills tingling.

"What is it?" Mason asked her.

She turned toward the group. Her daughter's widened green eyes stared at her from under the blanket. Emma couldn't frighten her already traumatized daughter. "Nothing. Let's go inside."

Constable Lucas nodded and held the door for them to enter.

Mason turned and gazed into the large front yard.

Had he sensed they were being watched, too?

He stepped over the threshold. "Constable, secure the perimeter," he whispered before walking farther into the house.

He *had* felt the trepidation as well.

The constable stepped back outside.

Tremors attacked her body, turning her veins to ice as a question ricocheted through her brain.

Would they ever be safe from the Luthers' clutches?

She sent up a prayer and followed the group into the farmhouse. The former owners had transformed the older home into a modern open concept, joining the kitchen and living room area together in perfect harmony. The furniture still held a farm feel. There were hardwood floors throughout. Gingham print–covered sofa and chairs with a rustic antique trunk, serving as a coffee table, sat in the living room. Green kitchen cupboards with white doorknobs matched the classic cast iron range. A sense of home washed over Emma, removing her earlier apprehension.

Mason set Sierra onto the couch and played another quick game of peekaboo. She giggled.

A sound Emma loved.

She walked to the window, pushing the green gingham drapes open a crack. Constable Lucas spoke into his radio from the front veranda. Probably to another officer stationed somewhere in the vicinity.

Emma didn't think all witnesses received this much protection. Not from what she'd seen on TV. However, she also knew better than to believe television.

She was living out her worst nightmare right now.

Isolated from everyone she loved.

God, I need You to show me why You blindsided me with all this.

Her tummy growled.

Not the response she wanted, but it prompted her to think about getting something to eat for Sierra. Emma's appetite had lessened in the past few days. She turned to Mason. "Time for supper?"

He stood. "I'll check the kitchen and cook you ladies something. I'm sure Dad's team bought groceries."

She tilted her head. "You cook?"

"Why are you so surprised?"

"Brady hated—"

"I'm not my brother." His rigid tone resonated in the cozy room.

She had to stop comparing them. "Sorry." But how could she not when they looked and sounded so much alike? She just prayed Mason didn't have Brady's temper. Her daughter's life was in this man's hands, and Emma wouldn't let anything threaten Sierra's safety.

A younger woman dressed in jeans and a plaid shirt entered the room. "We're all set up." She removed her round black glasses and inserted them in her shirt pocket.

Mason's hand flew to his sidearm. "Who are you?"

Emma grabbed his arm. "Relax, this is Tracey Smith. Your father's tech support person."

"Sorry." Mason dropped his hand by his side. "Did Dad also have someone stock the kitchen?"

"Sure did," Tracey said. "He also asked I bring you a police-issued laptop with secure connections. It's on the table." She turned to Emma. "Stocked you with candies, too. You doing okay?"

"Yes. How's your son, Cody?"

Tracey gathered her equipment and stuffed it in her bag. "Good. He's finally getting decent marks in second grade." She flung the knapsack over her shoulder. "Gotta run. Stay safe, Emma." She nodded to Mason and left the house.

"She's interesting," Mason said.

"You've never met her before?"

"Undercover work has put me out of the picture." He gestured to the hall. "Why don't you check out the bedrooms? I'll get supper ready."

An hour later, after Emma tucked Sierra into bed, she walked to the kitchen.

Mason's pinched expression stopped her midstep. Something had happened.

A jitter scampered over her skin, raising her guard. She approached and placed her hand on his shoulder. The simple contact sent a sizzling bolt up her arm.

He flinched.

She snapped her hand back. "What's wrong?" She held her breath, waiting for his response. *Please don't make us move again.*

"Dad told me earlier the SUV that chased me on the bridge and followed us is registered to my informant. I tried to find out more information on the computer but was unsuccessful." Mason slammed his laptop shut, his shoulders slouching. "I don't understand. He's helped me with different leads for years now and has never sold me out."

Emma sat opposite him, distancing herself. "Could someone have stolen it? Set him up?"

"Possibly." He paused. "Or the Luthers got to him."

She recoiled. The name only brought anguish

whenever she heard it. "Nothing about that family would surprise me. Their roots run deep."

Mason reopened the laptop and wiggled his computer mouse, bringing his screen to life. "Can you tell me about your takedown of their organization? I want to take notes."

"You assume they're behind all this?"

"Who else would it be?" He typed. "There's a mole somewhere within the witness protection program, so I will require all the names of your team members. I want to find out who's protecting each one."

She pointed to the laptop. "Are you sure it's safe? Hackers can access systems easily."

"It's secure. Dad made sure of it. Apparently, Tracey is the best."

But was she also easily bought? The Luthers were ruthless. However, Emma had to trust her father-in-law's judgment.

She leaned back. "I worked with a fellow CBSA officer—Heath Allen. US border officer Katrina Arnold, and some Buffalo police. Mainly narcotics officer Jason Moore."

Mason typed. "Tell me about Lincoln Luther."

Emma clamped her mouth shut. She envisioned the seventy-year-old's smug expression throughout the trial. No matter what evidence lawyers presented, he always wore the same sinister sneer. Like he knew he'd be released one day.

A tremble rattled through her. "He gives me

the creeps. He sat in his chair with a pleased look on his face—even after the jury convicted him."

"Has his lawyer filed an appeal?"

"Of course. His children are pressing the court to reopen his case on the grounds of insufficient evidence, when it was rock-solid. Lawyers warned the team we may need to be available again, so it was another push for me to enter the WPP."

"What do you know about Lincoln's company, Luther Shipping?"

Emma searched her memory bank of the crime father's business. "Family-run for three generations. His grandfather started it just after the First World War. He'd been injured and could no longer serve in the army, so he decided to give back by helping ship supplies overseas. Their reputation quickly put them at the top of the shipping industry, and the company profited."

"So, it began as a legitimate business?"

"Yes, but once Lincoln's father took over, everything changed."

Mason sat upright. "How?"

"I read an exposé on the Luther family, and suspicions mounted when Josiah Luther was seen hanging around various mob leaders." Emma massaged her tightened scalp. "However, no one could ever prove anything."

"Figures." Mason rubbed his brow with his thumb and index finger. "Tell me about the son."

"Lance Luther. Thirty-five years old. Married

with two young children. Claims someone framed his father."

Mason whistled. "Do you think that's possible?"

"Highly doubt it. The witnesses testified under oath that he hired them to smuggle the goods from Niagara Falls."

"Did they catch the dealers at the falls?" he asked.

Emma stood, walked over to the window and pulled the drapes open a crack. The clouds had finally broken, and the stars glittered alongside the glowing moon. She longed to be on a campsite, peering up at the sky with a roaring fire crackling. One of her favorite spots during summer. "No, they went into hiding. No one seems to know where. Officer Moore set up a sting, but they evaded the net." A tire hung on an enormous maple tree in the farmhouse's front yard. She would have to swing Sierra on it tomorrow.

"How did Lincoln get convicted?"

She turned from her peaceful trance. "Someone within his organization provided us documentation."

"Do you know who?"

She shook her head. "Whoever it was is now in WITSEC."

Mason once again typed on the laptop's keyboard. "What about Lincoln's daughter?"

"Layla Luther. Forty years old. Single. She cut off all ties to the Luther family. Took her inheritance and launched a nonprofit organization to help battered women. Layla's Centre of Hope."

"Could it be a front for something else?"

Emma walked to the fridge and pulled out a bottle of water. "She seems sincere in any news conference I've seen her in. Her passion for abused women is admirable."

"Makes you wonder if she's speaking from experience."

"Hard—"

A scream sounded from Sierra's bedroom, followed by a thud.

"Sierra!" Emma dropped her bottle and raced toward her daughter. She shouldn't have left her alone so soon after their arrival. What if someone entered the house from the rear? Hundreds of scenarios scrambled through her mind. *Lord, please keep my baby safe.*

Mason followed, and their footsteps hammered on the hardwood floor.

Emma threw open the door and flipped on the light.

Sierra lay huddled on the floor, sobbing.

Emma gathered her daughter in her arms. "Baby girl, what's wrong?"

"Bad man."

Mason knelt beside them. "Where, Sisi?"

Emma stiffened.

The name Brady used to call their daughter. She

had wiped the nickname from her mind ever since his death. It brought too much pain.

Sierra pointed to the window. "There."

Mason stood and reached for his holster. "I'll investigate." He left the room.

Emma lifted her daughter and brought her back to the bed. "Did you have a bad dream?"

Sierra nodded, a fat tear escaping down her cheek. "Yes, Mama."

Emma hugged her child and rocked her. "Baby girl, it's just a dream. You're safe."

Sierra wiggled over. "Mama, sleep with me."

Emma crawled under the covers. She picked up Jerome and tucked him between them. "There. We're all protected now."

"Ya-Y'ncle 'ason catch bad man. Like Daddy?"

Brady had also been a police officer. Seemed the force ran in the Jameses' bloodline. The fact that Sierra remembered surprised Emma.

"Yes, sweetie. Uncle Mason will catch them." Emma hoped. "Close your eyes. Time to sleep."

"Sing, Mama."

Emma sang her daughter's favorite lullaby that Brady had taught them from his childhood, and within minutes, Sierra was sound asleep. Emma waited a bit before sneaking out from under the covers and went back to the kitchen.

Mason entered the house. "She asleep?"

"Yes. Did you see anything suspicious? Please tell me we don't have to leave."

"No. I'm not sure what Sierra thinks she saw, but I checked with Constable Nash. He said no one has been around since the other constable left. I also scoured the perimeter. Nothing. No footprints outside her window." He removed his leather jacket, hanging it on the coatrack. "I'm curious. Why isn't Sierra's vocabulary more advanced? Shouldn't a four-year-old be able to form complete sentences?"

Emma figured he'd ask. Everyone who met her daughter did. "She was only one when Brady died, but his absence in her life affected her growth. She didn't progress like other children. I took her to a speech-language pathologist. She thought Sierra's issue was emotional from the loss of her father. I've been working on helping her ever since, and she's slowly gaining ground."

"I'm sorry his death took such a toll on her. I should have—"

An alarm shrieked.

Emma's legs wobbled, and she teetered.

Mason rushed forward and caught her. "What was that?"

She waved her arm, revealing a watch-type device, then checked the displayed numbers. "My CGM telling me my blood sugars are out of whack." Her continuous glucose monitor had been a lifesaver, reading her levels day and night. "I have eaten little today. I should know better."

He guided her to the chair. "What do you need?"

She pointed to the coffee table in the living room.

"My kit. I'll do a reading to ensure it matches and then inject myself."

He hustled over and grabbed her bag.

After pricking her finger and confirming the CGM's reading was correct, she injected herself with the appropriate amount of insulin. "Can you grab me some orange juice? Your father knows what to stock for me just in case."

Mason nodded and brought it to her. "Anything to eat?"

She took a sip. "I have something." She pulled a candy bar from her pocket, unwrapped the treat and stuck it in her mouth—a diabetic's saving grace. "I need…"

Nausea rose, and the room spun.

Mason called out to her, but his handsome face blurred.

She grabbed the chair's sides to steady herself. Flashing spots swam in her vision. Somewhere in the recesses of her mind, she heard Mason calling her name again.

What was happening?

Her heart pounded, and her nerve endings sparked, sending jolts of pain through her body. What had the Luthers done to her? A thought niggled in her foggy brain.

Her insulin. They had tampered with her insulin.

Before she could voice the concern, a blanket of darkness enveloped her, and she plunged into the abyss of nothingness.

THREE

"Emma!" Mason grabbed her as she began to sway and pulled her securely into his arms before sitting on the floor. He cradled her head. "Can you hear me?"

Silence.

He checked for a pulse. Faint.

Then he eyed her insulin bag. Had someone messed with her meds? Or had her CGM's reading been incorrect and she injected too much into her system? Either way, he had to get her to a hospital, but he trusted no one.

An idea formed.

Mason tugged his cell phone from his pocket and punched in his dad's number.

"Son, what's going on?"

"Emma fainted just after she took her insulin."

"Is she okay? What happened?" His father's anxious tone revealed his concern.

"I'll tell you more when I see you. Her pulse is weak. I don't trust Sierra's safety with anyone but you. Can you meet me at Jeff's hospital?"

"Wouldn't 911 be faster?"

"We're not far, and as I just said, I don't trust anyone, Dad. Inform Constable Nash we're leaving, but don't tell him where we're going."

"Got it. See you soon."

Seven minutes later, Mason turned the vehicle's lights and siren on before speeding from the driveway with Sierra wrapped in a blanket in her car seat and Emma slouched in the front seat. Her insulin bottle was tucked in his pocket. He struggled with announcing their presence, but it was vital they get to the hospital quickly.

After syncing his Bluetooth to the vehicle, he punched in Jeff's number.

"Dr. Thompson here."

"Jeff. It's Mason. I need your help."

"Mason, buddy, haven't heard from you in ages. What gives?" His best friend's voice was filled with agitation.

"Long story. Are you working right now?"

"Yes. Why?"

Mason took a sharp right turn onto the highway that would take him to the hospital. "I'm bringing my sister-in-law in. She's diabetic, and I think someone poisoned her insulin. I only trust you to work on her."

His friend sucked in a breath. "What's going on?"

"Will explain later. Please put Emma on your records as Kailey Brown. I realize this is a huge ask and unorthodox, but I'm out of options. Meet me at the emergency entrance. Be there in ten." He punched off and accelerated. He hoped he didn't sound rude, but Emma's health was his primary concern.

Dr. Thompson waved at Mason from the hospital's front doors ten minutes later. He stood beside a nurse clutching a gurney. A question plagued Mason's mind.

Could he trust them both?

Jeff has always been there for you, Mason.

He knew in his gut that his best friend would never betray him, but Mason prayed Jeff trusted this nurse. Emma and Sierra's safety depended on their discretion.

He jumped out of the vehicle and raced around to Emma. Jeff immediately pushed the gurney forward. Mason hesitated and eyed the petite woman.

Jeff squeezed Mason's arm. "Good to see you," he whispered. "I've put Emma in under Kailey Brown, as you requested. Nurse Atkins knows to keep this confidential, but that's all I told her."

Mason nodded. "Thank you. I'll tell you more later. Right now, let's get Em—Kailey inside." He lifted Emma from the car and onto the gurney just as a sedan pulled into a parking spot near them.

Chief Superintendent Seth James stepped out and approached the group. "Hey, Jeff. Been a while." He switched his focus to Mason. "Son, where's my granddaughter?"

He pointed. "Back seat. Can you get her? I'm going inside with Dr. Thompson and Kailey."

His father held out his hand. "Give me your

keys. I'll move the car and bring Tiddlywinks in with me."

Mason fished the key fob from his pocket and handed it over. "See you inside."

His dad grabbed his arm. "Wait. Did you bring her insulin? I'll get a constable to take it to Forensics to check it for poison."

"Right." Mason removed the vial and gave it to his father before following Nurse Atkins and Jeff into the hospital. They wheeled Emma past the emergency reception window.

Jeff directed the nurse into a room at the end of the hall, near the fire exit.

Off the beaten path.

Good thinking, buddy.

The duo immediately hooked Emma up to machines, and the nurse took vials of blood.

"Please walk these samples down to the lab yourself, Terri. Tell them we need results yesterday," Jeff said as he hooked up the IV line.

The nurse nodded and hurried from the room.

Mason stood on the other side of Emma's hospital bed. "Thank you for helping, Jeff."

"Mason, you know I'd do anything for you. You saved my life all those years ago, but what's going on?" The tall, blond doctor read Emma's vitals on the monitor.

Mason darted to the entrance and closed the door. "This stays between us, promise?"

"Of course."

Mason couldn't divulge everything about her case, but his friend deserved some answers. "Emma helped bring down a notorious crime family. They've targeted her, and I need to keep her safe."

Jeff's eyes bulged. "Oh my. And now I'm guessing she's in the WPP. That's why you called her Kailey."

"That's all I can say. I'm pretty sure someone tampered with her insulin. Dad is getting Forensics involved."

"The lab will check her blood as well."

Mason's cell phone buzzed, and he read the screen. His father asking for their room number. Mason texted the information back. "Dad is on his way here with Emma's daughter. We need them close by for protection, too."

"Understood." He typed on the portable computer. "Her vitals are weak, but she's holding her own right now. Until we know what we're facing, we'll monitor everything."

A knock sounded, and Mason opened the door.

His father entered, holding a sleeping Sierra.

He pointed to the only chair in the room. "We're waiting for blood results."

The older man sat and cradled Sierra in his arms, eyeing Jeff.

"I explained Emma was targeted, so we need to keep her identity a secret, Dad."

"Mr. James, I promise I'll use the utmost discretion with Emma's case. We've logged her in as Kailey Brown." Jeff took another reading off the monitor and entered the information into the system.

Mason's father shifted in his seat. "Thank you, Jeff. We appreciate your help." He turned to his son. "I have officers securing the perimeter. I handpicked them myself. I sent one back to the station to take the insulin to Forensics."

"Good. Thankfully, Sierra is out like a light."

The chief superintendent chuckled and kissed his granddaughter's forehead. "She's a doll."

"I'm going to check in with the lab to expedite the results. She's stable at the moment." Jeff left the room.

"How did you let this happen, Mason?" His father's eyes, which had softened earlier, now narrowed, showing disdain.

Mason's chest tightened. He couldn't win.

Nothing has changed, has it, Dad? Brady is still your favorite even though he's gone.

"We don't know yet. And how can you blame me for this?"

"You should have watched her closer." He peered down at Sierra. "Now Tiddlywinks may lose her mother, too."

Mason tightened his arms, cementing them at his side. He wanted to punch a hole in the wall, but losing control of his emotions wouldn't help Emma's condition or his father's opinion of him.

Brady, even in death, you still outshine me.

His brother had always hated the way their father treated Mason and stood up for his sibling.

I miss you, bro.

The last words he spoke to Brady rolled through his head. His brother had complained about a fight he'd had with Emma. Frustration from Mason's ended relationship with Zoe Dickerson had still been fresh, so he'd blurted out the first thing that came to mind.

"Bro, at least you have a loving wife. Stop complaining and pull up your britches and apologize."

Moments later, Mason heard tires squealing and a horrifying crash. He'd been on the phone with Brady when he died. A memory he wanted to erase.

Forever.

A mistake he wished he could go back and fix.

"Well, are you going to tell me what happened or not?" His father's question boomed in the small room, thrusting Mason back into the present.

He raked his fingers through his short hair. "I suspect someone tampered with her insulin. This is not my fault." His words seethed through his teeth.

"Mason, you need—"

Emma's monitor screeched rapid beats before slowing and turning to a deafening, flatlining beep.

No! Lord, don't take her, too.

Mason couldn't bear to lose his brother's wife.

* * *

Muffled noises sounded in the distance in a tunnel-like effect, and Emma struggled to clear her fuzzy brain. *What happened?*

"Kailey, can you hear me?" a male voice asked. *Where am I? Who's Kailey?*

She swallowed and winced at the sensation of glass-like slivers sliding down her throat.

Someone rubbed her arm. "It's Mason. Can you hear us?"

Mason? She turned her head and forced her eyes open. His blurry, handsome face slowly came into focus. Her shoulders relaxed at the sight of him. She was safe.

She glanced around the small room. A doctor wrote on a clipboard while a petite nurse spoke in hushed tones to him.

Right. Kailey was her WPP name. She searched her memory bank's last recollection she could find. She'd just taken her insulin and—

Her muscles clenched, and she tried to sit up.

Strong arms held her down. "Kailey, you need to remain calm." Mason's baritone voice enveloped her.

Stay calm? Someone had poisoned her insulin. It was the only answer. "S-i-e-r-r-a." Her daughter's name came out in a raspy stutter. Her weighted chest threatened to explode.

"She's okay. Don't worry, Dad is taking care of Sisi."

She expelled the breath she'd been holding, the pressure in her chest lightening. *Thank You, Lord.*

Emma grabbed Mason's arm. "My insulin. What happened?"

"I can answer that." A tall, slender man dressed in a white coat adjusted her IV. He dismissed the nurse. "I'm Dr. Jeff Thompson. Our lab found traces of fentanyl in your blood, and I'm guessing your Forensics department will also find it in your insulin. Thankfully, Mason got you here quickly."

"But it didn't kill me. Why?"

Once again, Mason rubbed her arm. "It did. Your heart stopped beating."

"What?"

"Yes," Dr. Thompson said. "Emma, God looked after you."

She glanced at Mason. "Wait, he didn't call me Kailey."

"Jeff is my best friend. I had to trust him. Your life depended on it."

The doctor clicked his pen and stuffed it into his front pocket. "Don't worry, I've logged everything under your WPP identity. And I'm the only one in the hospital who knows the truth." His cell phone rang, and he checked the screen. "I gotta tend to another patient. I'll be back." He left the room.

Emma bit her lip. "Why didn't I die, Mason?"

"Jeff would say God restarted your heart, because he told me they stopped compressions. Apparently, he even called your time of death. You were gone. Then your heart started."

Thank You, God.

The Luthers had come close to taking her out, but fortunately she'd been spared. "Lincoln Luther is responsible for this, but how did he get to me? I have to get out of the hospital. Now."

Once again, she tried to sit but fell back. Her weakened muscles zapped her energy.

"Calm down, Emma. You're safe. Dad has officers patrolling the area. Plus, he's down the hall with Sierra."

"Is the farmhouse compromised?"

"There's no indication of that. Constable Nash told Dad the area has been quiet."

"Well, then, how did they get to me?"

Mason rubbed his stubbled chin. "They got to your insulin somehow. Have you ever left your diabetic bag unattended?"

"No. It's always been in my possession or at the safe house."

His eyes widened. "That confirms we have a mole somewhere on Dad's team. But who? He's personally vetted everyone."

Emma's heart fluttered, increasing her rhythm. The monitor bleeped in quick, short dings, warning them of her panic. "I must see Sierra and get out of here, Mason."

"Take deep breaths. You need to remain still.

Sierra is fine. I'll text Dad." He pulled out his cell phone and keyed a message.

She breathed in and out, slowly calming her pulse. *You've got this, girl.*

Moments later, the door opened and Seth James walked in with a sleeping Sierra cradled over his shoulder.

Emma looked upward and thanked God for keeping her and her daughter safe. She raised her arms. "Can I have her in bed with me?"

Seth kissed Sierra's forehead before placing Emma's daughter into her arms.

"My sweet baby girl. Mama is here."

Sierra stirred but snuggled closer as if sensing her mother's presence.

Emma's muscles quivered, and she held her little girl tighter. "We need to find out who's doing this." Her elevated tone surprised even herself, but she couldn't help it. Her daughter's life was at stake, and Emma would do anything to keep Sierra safe.

"We will. I promise." Seth turned to Mason. "Right, son?" The anger in his voice was undeniable and almost held a threat toward his son.

Emma knew the battle they tried so hard to hide from everyone around them, but Brady had told her the truth. Mason struggled to live up to his father's standards, and Seth pushed his son to be the best. Too much.

Mason cleared his throat. "I promise, I'll—"

A high-pitched squeal sounded, interrupting the

conversation. "Your attention, please. Code black. A1 205, ICU." The female announcer repeated the message two more times. Her shaky voice conveyed her trepidation.

Seth pulled out his cell phone. "That's a bomb threat! I'm calling in a team. Stat." He turned his back to them and spoke in hushed tones.

Once again, Emma's pulse quickened. She held Sierra tighter in her embrace, vowing to protect her from whatever was ahead of them.

Seconds later, Dr. Thompson burst through the door. "We need to get Emma out of here. Now. This isn't a drill."

"Jeff, is she strong enough?" Mason asked.

"She's too weak to stand, so we'll wheel her out on the bed. The nurse at the emergency entrance found a suspicious package. We called the threat in and need to evacuate."

Seth punched off his call. "K-9 dog and bomb unit are en route."

The doctor unhooked her monitor and pushed the IV stand toward Seth. "Sir, can you maneuver this?" He turned to Mason. "Let's move."

They ran through the corridor along with all other patients and hospital staff.

The commotion woke Sierra, and she wailed. Emma clutched her even closer. "Hang on, baby girl. Mama's got you."

"Mama!" Sierra wrapped her arms around her mother's neck, squeezing.

They bolted through the doors. The warm summer breeze hit Emma's face. The pandemonium of other patients' screams elevated her daughter's wail. Emma sang into Sierra's ear.

"Mason, I need to go check on other patients." Dr. Thompson hurried back into the building without waiting for Mason's reply.

Mason wheeled Emma's bed to the side of the building. Both he and Seth flanked her, resting a hand on their weapons.

Did they suspect something?

Within minutes, the bomb unit and K-9 arrived, and the officers conferred with Seth before entering the building.

Jeff raced back to the group. "We've evacuated the unit."

Seth's cell phone rang a few moments later. "James here." A pause. "What? Are you sure?" His gaze snapped to Mason's.

The hairs on Emma's neck prickled.

"Thanks for confirming." Seth clicked off. "K-9 dog did not find a bomb in the package. We need to get back inside. Right now."

Seth and Mason pulled their weapons simultaneously, raising them before shielding Emma and Sierra.

A shiver coiled up her spine, sending fear permeating throughout her body. Was it a trap to get them outside?

A bullet blasted the pavement in answer to her unspoken question.

Someone had found them.

Again.

FOUR

"Emma, quick. Pull your legs up!" Mason grabbed the railing and jumped up on the end of her hospital bed, keeping his weapon raised. He needed to shield her and Sierra. The urge to protect them with his life by placing himself in front of them was the only answer, and he didn't hesitate. "Dad, cover us. Jeff, get us inside."

His best friend moved to the head of the bed and pushed them toward the entrance while trying to maneuver the IV line. A patient-care assistant noticed and grabbed the pole to assist.

An explosion sounded somewhere nearby, moments before the hospital's power snapped off. Seconds later, multiple shots rang out, hitting the streetlights and plunging them into a blackout.

They were blindsided.

Screams from other patients and staff flooded the darkened area, increasing the panic growing around them.

His father yelled orders into his cell phone to other officers in the area, pointing his Smith & Wesson wherever he thought the shot had come from.

More sirens and flashing lights approached at

full speed and illuminated the dimmed hospital's entrance. Officers jumped out of their cruisers.

"Shots came from that angle." His dad pointed across the street. "Find the shooter."

The team scrambled to obey his gruff order with their rifles pointing in every direction.

Jeff pushed Emma's bed into the hospital, down the hall and back into her room.

Sierra whimpered even though Emma had her cradled in her arms.

Mason hopped off the bed and holstered his weapon. "Emma, you okay?"

She nodded, but her terror-stricken eyes told him differently.

The bomb threat had taken its toll.

Mason tugged at Jeff's arm. "Can I talk to you in the hall?"

They left the room.

"I need to get Emma back to the safe house. Is it healthy to transport her?"

Jeff crossed his arms. "Not a good idea. She just woke up."

He understood his friend's concern but had to convince him to discharge Emma. "The bomb threat was a ruse to get us outside to kill Emma. She's not protected here. Please."

"It's against my better judgment, but let me check her vitals again, and then I'll decide." He walked into the room and rehooked Emma to the monitor.

Thankfully, Sierra had fallen back asleep in her mother's arms.

Thank You, God.

The quick prayer startled him. Was he talking to God now? It had been years since he even thought about trusting in the One who stole his mother from Mason in such a heart-wrenching way. Her murder still plagued him after ten years.

"What do you mean, you *lost* them?"

Seth James's raised voice snapped Mason back to the present.

His father glanced at Mason. "I gotta go. Keep me updated." He clicked off.

"What's going on, Dad?"

"They lost the suspect, and the vehicle had no plates."

Too many dead ends. "Probably stolen anyway. Listen, I've asked Jeff to release Emma. She's not safe at the hospital. I have no idea how they tracked her here."

Emma raised her hand. "I'm here and can speak for myself. I want to leave. We're too exposed."

"Agreed. I've contacted Constable Lucas to meet us here. Once Jeff gives the green light, Tom will escort you back to the farmhouse."

He nodded. "Where are you going?"

"To my home office. I need to do some digging. I'll keep you updated."

Mason looked back at Emma. Her ashen face

revealed her weakened state, but they couldn't stay at the hospital.

Jeff approached. "I don't know, Mason. I'm not comfortable releasing her. She's still weak."

"I'll be fine, Dr. Thompson," Emma said.

The thought of something else happening to Emma quickened Mason's pulse. He needed to fulfill the promise he'd made to Brady—protect his family. "Jeff, if her condition worsens, you'll be the first we call."

"He's right, Jeff," Mason's dad said. "Discharge her and I won't take no for an answer."

Great, that's all they needed. His father's stubborn and rough disposition was only making a bad situation worse. Mason had to smooth the waters. "We realize this is a big ask. I get that you're responsible for your patient, but you've seen how ruthless these people can be. They will stop at nothing to get to her. I owe it to my brother to protect them."

"I can take care of myself, Mason," Emma said.

Mason raised his hands in a stop position. "I know, Em, but Brady would want me to pull out all stops to keep you and Sisi safe."

She opened her mouth to speak but stopped, her face twisting with emotion.

Something about her shift in demeanor at the mention of Brady nagged him, but he couldn't put his finger on what appeared to trouble his sister-in-law.

She kissed Sierra's forehead. "Dr. Thompson, Mason is right. I'm okay to move back to the safe house. For my daughter's sake, please discharge me."

Jeff let out an elongated, audible sigh. "Fine." He waggled his finger in Mason's face. "But you call me if anything changes in her condition."

"Absolutely," he said.

A knock sounded, and Mason eased open the door.

Constable Lucas.

Mason stepped into the hall. "Thanks for coming. Can you check our vehicle for any trackers?" He handed Lucas the key fob.

"You suspect that's how they found Emma here?"

"It has to be. I need to be sure before we head back."

The constable nodded and left.

Ten minutes later, Lucas returned and reported the car was free from any tracking devices.

What? Mason muzzled a growl, frustration setting in at the question of how they knew their location. He would take an alternate route back to the farmhouse. Just in case.

After getting Emma set up in the king-size bed in her room with Sierra an hour later, he went back to work on the laptop Tracey had provided. He wanted to do further research on all the names Emma gave him, plus the Luthers. The more he could discover, the better he'd be able to understand the way they thought. If that was possible with the notorious crime family.

Mason had ensured no one followed them on their way back to the safe house other than Constable Lucas. Lucas now replaced Constable Nash and sat outside in his unmarked cruiser.

Singing drew Mason's attention.

He tiptoed down the hall, the sound luring him like a mermaid to the sea. He peeked around the entrance of Emma's room.

She had tucked the little girl into bed and was snuggled beside her. Emma's sweet voice filled the air as she sang to Sierra.

Mason placed his hand over his mouth to stop the choke wanting to expel. His mother used to sing the same lullaby to him and Brady when they were young. The song had lulled them from an agitated state to stillness.

Sierra yawned.

The song had the same impact today.

Mason leaned on the door frame, enjoying Emma's beautiful voice. The scene held him in a trance, and he wanted this moment to last. Their confrontation earlier in the day still riled him. He should never have asked her how she was doing with everything.

Too soon, Mason.

He needed to rebuild their relationship. One step at a time.

Being in Emma and Sierra's presence for the past few hours solidified his commitment to do just that. A phrase his mother used to say swept through his mind.

Repair the past to have a future.

Could he? Or more importantly…

Did he want to?

Sierra's gaze turned in his direction. She raised her little arms and wiggled her fingers, beckoning him forward. "Hug, Ya-Y'ncle 'ason?"

The way she attempted to say his name touched his heart and answered his unspoken question.

Yes, he wanted to be a part of Sierra's and Emma's lives, but his protective nature wouldn't allow him to get too close. His priority was to ensure they stayed safe, and if his cover had been blown, he couldn't put them in more danger.

He approached the bed and sat.

The little girl lunged forward and wrapped her arms around his neck. "Nighty."

"Don't let the bedbugs bite," he said.

Sierra popped back. "Bugs? Mama?"

Emma eyed him.

Awkward.

Nice, Mason. Face it, you don't know how to handle a four-year-old. Criminals, yes, but a child?

He longed to be a father one day. Clearly, he had a lot to learn.

Emma snuggled closer. "Baby girl, he's kidding. There are no bugs in our bed. Sleep time." She turned her gaze toward him. "Go to bed, Mason. It's 3:00 a.m."

He was too wired to sleep. "Do you need anything?"

She shook her head. "Are we safe?"

"Constable Lucas is outside, and there's no one around. We're good. Night."

He backed out of the room and closed the door. Then walked to the living room window and peered into the darkness. Lucas was leaning against the cruiser, his cell phone glowing as he tapped the keys. Sighing, Mason surveyed the secluded farmhouse grounds, looking for potential threats. The overpowering desire to shield Emma and Sierra from harm haunted him.

His fear of failing as a protector resurfaced and sent trepidation gouging his chest. He inhaled. *You can do this, Mason.*

He had to. There was no other option.

Emma woke to her daughter singing her favorite song again, "You Are My Sunshine." Brady had sung it to Sierra every night before bed. Had the little girl remembered his voice from so long ago? Tears stung, and she swallowed. Tears not from the loss of her husband, but the loss of what he used to be. Or at least of who she'd *thought* he was. A year into their marriage, a man filled with unbridled rage had replaced the kind, loving man she'd said "I do" to. Brady's abuse started one night when she returned home late from work and escalated from there. His love quickly turned into obsession, and she couldn't escape his blows.

"Mama. Get up. I'm hungry." Sierra shoved Jerome into Emma's face, suspending thoughts of the little girl's father.

Yesterday's incident had taken more out of her than she cared to admit, but for her daughter's well-being, she forced her weary limbs to move. "Give me a minute, baby girl. Mama's tired."

"I go see Ya-Y'ncle 'ason." She whipped off the covers and hopped out of bed. Her little feet pattered on the hardwood floor.

"Slow down, Sierra. He might be asleep."

Her daughter shot out of the room and yelled Mason's name. Emma chuckled, her heart warming at the idea of another male role model in Sierra's life. Her hand flew to her mouth. No, Mason had proved over the last few years he wasn't capable of having a relationship with his niece. She couldn't let Sierra get used to the idea of having him around, even if Emma wanted him nearby. Wait—

Had she just thought that? She *was* tired.

She eased herself into a seated position. Baby steps. However, her body required something to eat. She didn't want her sugars to get erratic again. Thankfully, Dr. Thompson had given her more insulin—poison-free. She'd racked her brain to figure out how someone had gotten to her medical bag, but nothing out of the ordinary came up.

She waited a minute before planting her feet onto the cool floor and stood. Her legs threatened to give out, and she grabbed the headboard. *You can do this.* She reached for her housecoat and wrapped the fuzzy robe around herself. Taking tiny steps, she made her way into the hall and down to the kitchen, hugging the wall.

And stopped at the sight before her.

Mason was dressed in gray-and-blue-plaid cotton pajama bottoms and a blue T-shirt, his firm muscles protruding as he jostled Sierra on his knee.

Her daughter giggled.

Emma squashed the cry wanting to escape. A memory flashed, of a younger Sisi sitting on Brady's knee smiling ear to ear when her father played a bouncing game.

The day before his death.

"Mama!"

Sierra's yell catapulted Emma back to the scene at hand. She shook off thoughts of Brady and stepped forward. "Morning, Mason."

He smirked. "Morning? It's one in the afternoon."

She leaned against the counter. "Wow. I can't believe I didn't wake earlier."

"Your body needed the rest. I'm surprised this one slept so long." Mason buried a playful zerbert into Sierra's neck.

Her daughter squirmed at the buzz of his lips on her skin. "Tickle."

"You two are obviously getting along fine. Did she wake you?"

Mason lifted Sierra and sat her in a chair. "Hardly. I've been doing some research into the Luthers. How are you feeling?"

"Weak. I need food."

He pulled out a chair. "Sit and I'll make you and Sierra a late breakfast."

An hour later, Emma propped herself up on the comfy sectional couch. Sierra played with a puzzle in the kitchen. Thankful for the open-concept layout, Emma leaned back and shut her eyes.

Mason walked into the room, holding his laptop. "Em, can you tell me a bit more about Lance Luther?"

Did he have to use that nickname? He'd called her that from the first time they'd met at church. They became friends and he soon asked her out, but she wasn't interested. Even though she'd felt an attraction to him, she hadn't liked his nonchalant attitude. Her best friend, Robin Bates, thought Emma was nuts for turning him down and said so. The fact that she later married his almost-twin brother made Robin question whether or not Emma had chosen the right brother. She, too, had challenged her own decision after Brady's first slap. Strange how things could change in a flash. Emma touched her cheek as if it still stung.

She opened her eyes and sat up. She glanced at Sierra and was thankful her daughter still immersed herself in the puzzle. "What do you want to know?"

"He opened his own business, right?" Mason glanced at the laptop screen. "A marketing firm?"

"Yes, why?"

"Why wouldn't he work for his father at Luther Shipping? I know little about the family's background. Do you?"

She pulled her legs up and hugged them to her chest. "He and Lincoln had a falling-out about how Lance felt his father should run the family business. They parted ways, and Lance started his own company."

"When was this?"

"Ten years ago."

"What is Lance's relationship with Layla like?" He clicked on the laptop and flipped the screen around. "They don't look too friendly in this picture."

Emma leaned closer for a better look. The brother and sister were attending a fundraiser for Layla's nonprofit organization. The picture captured Lance pointing his finger into Layla's face. "They do not get along. From the research into their family, I know they've had a shaky relationship since they were younger."

"How's Layla's relationship with her father?" he asked.

"Estranged ever since her mother died."

"Why do you think that is?"

Emma grabbed her tea from the coffee table and took a sip. "Jaclyn Luther died of a drug overdose when Layla was fifteen. Layla blamed her father and accused him of killing Jaclyn."

Mason whistled. "Does anyone in this family get along?"

"Not really. Layla accused Lance of framing his father to get him incarcerated. Not sure I believe that."

"If she didn't get along with Lincoln, why did she care?"

"Who knows?" She took another sip before returning her tea to the coffee table. Then pulled the afghan tighter around her legs. "Mason, can I ask you a question? I need you to be honest."

He closed his laptop. "That doesn't sound good. Sure. Shoot."

"Where have you really been for the past three years? Sierra needed you in her life. She was only a baby when Brady died, but his death still took a toll on her."

Mason blew a breath out and stood. He walked over to the window and peeked out.

Was he stalling or trying to make up an excuse?

"Dad demanded I stay away."

Emma flinched. *No way.*

Not the words she'd expected to come out of his mouth.

* * *

The wall clock chimed, intruding on their conversation. Mason could tell from the stilled silence that his confession had shocked Emma. She clearly only saw the tender grandfather side of Chief Superintendent Seth James. The man who loved his younger son deeply and doted on Emma and Sierra. However, Mason saw the gruff and rigid man who was tough on his staff. Unfortunately, Mason had fallen into that category. No matter what he did, his father never appeared to be proud of the work Mason had accomplished. Even receiving special recognition after solving a cold case in Nova Scotia hadn't helped Mason raise a notch in his father's service belt.

For years, he had struggled with winning his father's approval. However, when Seth requested Mason step away from contacting Emma, Mason had obliged. Another attempt to remedy their shaky relationship.

"I… I don't know what to say." Emma's stuttered words conveyed her disbelief.

"I'm not trying to put Dad in a poor light, but I wanted to be honest." A sudden urge to hold her in his arms to reassure her overwhelmed him, and he stuffed his hands under his legs to stifle the temptation.

He prided himself on honesty. Well, as much as he could with working undercover and the secrets that accompanied his cover. His life and others on his team depended on it.

"I never realized that. He's always sweet to us, even when Brady was alive."

Mason bit back the retort he wanted to say. He wouldn't badmouth his father. Even after everything he'd done, Mason loved him.

He just found it hard to respect him.

"I'm sorry. Dad is an amazing grandfather. Don't forget that. He loves his family deeply."

"He just doesn't show it with you. Why?"

Could he spill the truth about everything? About how Mason blamed his father for his mother's death? A high-profile case had put Seth in the spotlight, and Mason had warned his father to place his mother in a safe house, but his father refused—said only his life was at stake.

A day later, Mason found his mother shot, assassin-style, in their home. The suspect had posed as a delivery man to gain access.

Chief Superintendent Seth James's pride had gotten his wife killed.

Mason had never forgiven him for it.

"Mason?"

Emma's worried voice brought him back to the moment.

"You noticed there was tension between me and my dad?"

"Hard not to. I often asked Brady about it, but he would never tell me, and I'm not sure why."

She picked up her tea and ran her thumb around the rim.

"I loved my brother, but when it came to Dad, he turned a blind eye. Perhaps he never understood, as they had a strong relationship. Two peas in a pod—so to speak." He shrugged. He accepted the situation. Not that he liked it.

Besides Emma and Sierra, his father was the only family he had left. Mason longed to fix their relationship.

But could he ever forgive his dad for his part in their mother's death? Brady had begged Mason to let it go.

It's time.

His cell phone buzzed, preventing Mason from mulling over where that thought had come from. He checked the text.

Lance Luther spotted near Niagara Falls. Be on alert.

Had the son crossed the border into Canada to finish his father's work?

FIVE

Emma noted the tension in Mason's wrinkled forehead. Not good. Her pulse rocketed. *Please, Lord. I don't have the strength to run today.* "What's happening?"

"Dad warning me that Lance Luther was spotted in Niagara Falls." Mason got up and walked to the window. He parted the blinds and peered out.

Was he concerned Lance had already found them? Once again, her heart palpitated.

She glanced at Sierra to ensure her daughter's puzzle building still captured her attention. Thankfully, she was engrossed in fitting the pieces together. Similar to what Emma was trying to do in their lives. Putting the jigsaw back after being ripped from all her family and friends to hide in WPP. *Lord, please help me to see my sister and parents again. End this madness.*

She glanced at Mason. "Let's not panic. He has business clients here in Canada. That's probably all it is."

He turned from the window, crossing his arms. "I can't take that risk, Em."

She wished yet again that he'd stop calling her by Brady's nickname. The intimate name was thawing her frozen heart, and she couldn't go through more pain right now. Having to deal with her husband's abuse had scarred her from ever getting into another relationship for fear of becoming entangled with another angry, violent man. She refused to put herself or Sierra through that kind of upheaval again.

"Please don't make us run," she whispered. "I can't keep uprooting my daughter."

His hazel eyes softened. "Dad would never forgive me if something happened to either of you."

"Can't you get more police presence here instead? The Luthers aren't aware of our location." She fisted her hands. "I need this to be over." Tears welled, and she buried her face in her hands.

Mason rushed over and took her in his arms. "Shh. I've got you. It's gonna be okay."

She nestled into his embrace, liking how it felt to have his strong arms around her. It had been too long, and she hadn't realized until this moment how much she missed a man's embrace.

Mason is not Brady.

She prayed she could truly believe that sentiment.

Suddenly, her pent-up emotions from the past few weeks of being in WPP took over, and she sobbed. So much loss. Loss of family. Loss of friends. Loss of her identity.

Why, God, are You allowing this in our lives?

"Let it out, Em. I won't let anything happen to you or Sisi. I promise."

Could he guarantee that? She and Brady had kept tabs on his police career and she recognized he was good at his job, but no one was perfect.

The pitter-patter of little feet approached, interrupting her thoughts. "Mama? Hug?"

Emma pulled away from Mason and wiped her eyes. "Hey, baby girl. Mama's okay. Come here."

Mason moved from his position and lifted Sierra onto Emma's lap. "I'm going to go check with Constable Lucas outside. Be right back."

She nodded and hugged Sierra. "I love you, sweet Sisi."

"I wuf you, too."

Emma held her daughter and sang their special song—more for her than Sierra. A wave of peace washed over her, and her tension slowly dissipated. *You've got this*.

A ding from Mason's computer sounded as a thought raced through her mind. She needed to help him in the investigation. After all her research, she knew the Luthers the best.

Emma rolled her shoulders back, determination setting in on solving this case and putting all the Luthers out of their lives.

For good.

Then she and Sierra would be free to go home.

Home sounded *so* good.

Mason returned and locked the door behind him. "Constable Lucas is working with Dad to get more unmarked cruisers in the area. This will help protect you."

Emma released Sierra, and the four-year-old went back to her puzzle. "Thank you. Mason, I need to help with the investigation."

"You're still weak, Em. I don't need your blood pressure rising along with your glucose levels."

"I'll be fine," she insisted. "I know the Luthers better than you. I've been studying them for a long time. I can help. Plus, the work will keep my mind off things."

"Dad will have my head."

"You let me handle your father." She lifted the lid of his laptop. "Let's get started. I heard a notification come in while you were outside."

"You're not taking no for an answer, are you?"

His smirk caused her stomach to flutter. Emma put her hand on her tummy to quench the feelings emerging. *You can't go there.*

Emma ensured Sierra was still preoccupied before answering. "No, I'm not. What else do you need to know?"

Mason sat and hit the laptop's space bar. The screen came to life. "I'll check emails."

Emma grabbed the notebook he'd left on the coffee table and flipped the book open, reading down the list of questions he'd written. Were Lance's business dealings legit? Why did Layla start a nonprofit organization? And how come the siblings were estranged from their father?

If only she had the files with her notes and research she'd done while working on the case. Plus her laptop. They were all locked in her office filing cabinet at her house. The house she'd fled in the middle of the night weeks ago.

"Mason, is there any way someone can retrieve all my research and my laptop from my house? The files might help."

He tapped his finger on his chin. "Maybe Dad's computer geek can help."

"Tracey? She's not a geek! She's been very sweet, setting me up in the safe houses." She met his eyes. "But yes, I think you're right about her helping us. None of my neighbors know her, so they probably wouldn't suspect if she showed up there."

He pulled out his cell phone. "Maybe Dad can send her under a ruse of selling your home. If anyone asks, she could say you had to leave suddenly and won't be back. I'll get him on it right away."

Hope surged through Emma's body.

Perhaps this would be the start of the end of this madness.

Over the next day, while Mason waited for his father to get all the notes Emma had taken, they worked at piecing together a timeline of everything from border patrol stopping the drug-laced souvenirs to Lincoln Luther's arrest. Thankfully, no further Lance sightings were reported, but he had also not returned to the United States, so their guard remained elevated. To that end, Mason called an acquaintance in the Buffalo PD, and the officer confirmed Lance's office stated he was in Niagara Falls for a business meeting. However, Mason still suspected this wasn't the real reason he was MIA. Lance was clearly up to no good.

Dusk had settled in, and Mason snapped the end table light on as they searched social media for more Luther posts. So far, nothing had popped up.

He had also tried to get in touch with his informant Skip Perry. The man seemed to have vanished, but Mason put out feelers in the area.

Thankfully, the day's reprieve helped Emma regain some of her strength. Jeff called twice to check on her, and Mason assured him she had recovered nicely.

A knot settled in his stomach, convincing him another round of trouble wasn't far away. Mason often had these feelings when his intuition went into overdrive. And right now, he knew one thing with a hundred percent certainty.

He needed to stay on guard. At all times.

His cell phone buzzed, and he glanced at the number.

Unknown.

Mason could count on one hand the number of people who had his unlisted number. He hovered over the decline button, but after a couple seconds, he hit Answer. "Mason here."

"They're after me!" A frantic voice boomed in his ear.

He bolted off the couch. "Skip, where have you been?"

Emma looked up from reading his notebook, eyes widening.

"Hiding. They. Framed. Me. I did not betray you, Mason." His words came out rushed, as if he was running.

"Slow down. Why did someone use your vehicle to ram me on the Peace Bridge?"

"No idea. No one knows I'm your CI."

Had someone within the police force leaked to the Luthers Skip's confidential informant identity? A prickle raced up his back and settled in his neck, creating instantaneous tension.

Ragged spurts of breath sounded through his cell phone.

"Skip, why are you running?"

"They found me."

"Who?" he demanded.

"Not sure. A black SUV just tried to run me over after I left my apartment building. I need to see you. I have information about the Luthers."

Was this a ploy to get him away from Emma and Sierra? "Skip, I'll contact Dad. He'll get someone else. I can't leave right now."

"No! I will only deal with you. Don't. Trust. Anyone. But. You."

Skip wouldn't have betrayed him, and now he

was in trouble. He needed to get to his CI before it was too late.

A gunshot boomed through the phone.

"Skip! Skip!"

Nothing.

Had the Luthers taken out his CI?

"Skip?"

"I'm here. I had to hide. You need to protect me. You owe me that."

The man was right. He'd been a valuable source of information over the few years Mason had been back in Ontario. He couldn't let him down. "Tell me where you are."

"I'm heading to a friend's apartment." He rattled off the address.

Mason glanced at his watch. It would take him twenty minutes to get there. "Okay, take an alternate route. I'll come as quickly as possible. Stay safe."

"Hurry!" Skip clicked off.

Emma stood. "You can't leave us."

"I'm sorry. Skip will only talk to me and says he has information about the Luthers." Mason walked over to her and took her hands in his, ignoring the zap of electricity surging between them. He forced himself to focus on the here and now. "This could break the case wide-open and maybe you'll be able to return home."

He hated to make such a promise, but he had to give her a bit of hope.

She pulled her hands away. "I get it. We'll be fine. Can you ask your dad to send someone else to at least cover us here in the house?"

"Yes, he will—"

The doorbell interrupted his statement.

Who else knew their location?

Somehow, a caller had bypassed Lucas's surveillance.

Mason's muscles tautened. "Take Sierra into your bedroom. *Now!*" An intruder would probably never ring the doorbell, but he couldn't expose them.

She grabbed her daughter and ran down the hall.

Mason withdrew his nine-millimeter and positioned himself to the side of the door. "Who is it?"

"Mason, it's me."

Darlene, his partner.

"I'm here to help keep Emma safe while you go see Skip."

He flinched.

How did she know that? Was she the mole?

You've been partners with her for two years. She's trustworthy.

Then again, right now he didn't trust anyone but Emma and his father. He raised his gun and eased the door open a crack. "How did you find out about that so fast?"

She raised her hands. "Mason, relax. Didn't your dad tell you?"

"Tell me what?" *Dad, what are you keeping from me?*

"Let me in and I'll explain."

Mason hesitated. His cell phone buzzed. He removed it from his pocket with his free hand.

Holster your weapon and let Darlene in.

A thought niggled at him.

How did Dad know?

"Yes, Mason. Your dad is watching." Darlene pointed to the wall clock. "There's a camera in there."

His father had bugged the house.

Mason steeled his jaw. What else had the chief superintendent kept from him? Had his father heard all their conversations?

Questions he'd ask his father later. Mason holstered his gun and opened the door. "Sorry about that."

She stepped inside. "No worries. Glad you're cautious. Tom and I both thought you were aware."

Mason turned toward the clock. "Dad, you should have told me you were watching." Heat flushed his face and took up residence in his body. He had to control the anger, but this was obviously another case of his father not believing Mason could do his job.

"Emma, you can come out," he yelled.

Seconds later, the duo returned to the open-concept living area. "Hi, Darlene," Emma said.

His partner waved. "I'm here to keep you safe while Mason finds his CI."

Emma glanced at him, her twisted expression raising a question.

He pointed to the clock. "We're being watched."

"By who?" she demanded, her nostrils flaring.

"Dad."

She walked closer to the clock. "That's an invasion of privacy!"

"We'll get it removed when I get back." He grabbed his jacket from the coatrack. "I need to get to Skip before it's too late. Darlene will protect you, and Constable Lucas is outside."

She nodded.

Twenty minutes later, Mason pulled into the apartment complex Skip had mentioned. The dimly lit area revealed the run-down building deep in the center of the small town's homeless population. A steel drum to the right housed a roaring fire, its embers spitting into the sky. Several people huddled around the barrel to keep warm, even though the evening still held a trace of mugginess. These people each had a story of how they ended up living on the streets. Why did God allow their heartache?

Questions Mason realized he'd probably never know the answers to.

He should know. God put many detours in his own life.

An alley cat screeched nearby, and Mason shuddered.

Focus.

He discarded thoughts of God and entered the building, making his way to the apartment number Skip had given him. He knocked.

A shadow passed over the peephole.

"Skip, it's Mason," he whispered. "Let me in."

The door whipped open, and his CI tugged him inside. "Thank God you're here. Were you followed?"

"No." Mason surveyed the tiny apartment. Multiple newspapers covered the coffee table, along with various discarded pop cans. A pile of pizza boxes lined one wall. "Who lives here, Skip?"

"A friend from high school. She's at work right now."

"Tell me what's going on. I need to get back to my witness."

"A few days ago, I realized my SUV was missing. I'd been using my other vehicle and thought nothing of it, as my buddy drives the SUV often. He has an extra set of keys."

Mason put his hand on his hips. "For drug runs?"

"No comment. Anyway, when the vehicle wasn't returned, I reached out to my friend. He hadn't been using it. It had been stolen."

"And you didn't report it?"

"Would you?" Skip scoffed. "I'm a convicted felon, remember?"

He had a point. "Go on."

"I then heard they targeted you using my SUV."

Mason hooked his thumbs through his belt loops. "How would you know that?"

"You think I don't have my own contacts? Not sure how they tied us together, though."

Mason pulled a notebook from his back pocket. "So what information do you have on the Luthers?"

"Promise you won't get mad at me?"

Mason clenched his jaw. He didn't have time for this. "Just tell me."

"One of my dealers from the Buffalo area received inside information about a mole in the US marshals' office who's leaking witness locations."

"What information did he give you?"

Skip reached into his front jeans pocket. "Just a name. It's—"

The glass shattered, and Skip dropped to the floor. Bullet to the forehead.

Mason crouched and unleashed his weapon.

He waited for more gunfire, but none came. Mason felt for Skip's pulse. Nothing.

Clear intent that their target had been eliminated, wiping out Mason's first solid lead.

SIX

Not knowing whom to rely on in law enforcement, Mason reached out to the one person he didn't want to talk to but the only one he'd trust with Emma's life—Seth James. Mason explained the situation, and his father promised to send a team to his location. "One more thing, Dad. We need to talk. Meet me back at the farmhouse." He didn't wait for an answer and clicked off the call.

He glanced at Skip's body as a lump formed in Mason's throat. Guilt flowed through his veins at the loss of his best CI. Sure, the man had irritated Mason many times, but he always had Mason's back. "Skip, I'm so sorry. I—"

A paper peeked out from Skip's pocket. Mason recalled him reaching for something when the shot took his life.

He pulled the item out. A business card with a name in bold letters.

Deputy US Marshal Darryl Rollins.

Thoughts of this man being the mole tumbled through Mason's brain, but he stuffed the card into his pocket and concentrated on the immediate situation.

Mason arrived back at the farmhouse an hour later after consulting with his father's team. They'd secured the crime scene and would conduct the investigation.

Seth James's sedan sat in the driveway.

Mason's pulse pounded in his head. His father always managed to raise his blood pressure. He took a breath and exited the vehicle.

Time to confront his boss.

Mason stepped inside and stopped short at the sight before him. The tough superintendent bounced his granddaughter on his knee, singing "Jesus Loves Me."

When Sierra glanced up, she jumped off his dad's lap and raced over to hug Mason's legs.

"Y'ncle Mason. I wuf you."

Mason picked her up and twirled her around. "You said my name. I love you, too, Sisi."

His father cleared his throat. "Emma, can you take Sierra?"

Really, Dad? You can't let me have one moment with my niece?

Emma approached and mouthed the word *sorry* before taking Sierra from him. "Time for bed, baby girl."

"No, Mama." She squirmed in her mother's arms and reached for Mason.

"It's okay, Sisi. I'll see you in the morning." He kissed her forehead. "Night."

Her little lips quivered as plump tears emerged.

Mason wiped them with his thumb, melting the wall of ice he'd formed throughout the years.

He quenched the emotions rising within him and watched Emma and his niece disappear into the bedroom down the hall. The urge to be in Emma's and Sierra's lives tugged at his heart once again.

"Don't even think about it, Mason." His father's rough voice whispered deafening intent. "You can't get involved. They're off-limits."

Mason waggled a finger. "You have no right to tell me what to do after what you've done."

His dad stumbled backward. "I did it to protect Emma and my granddaughter."

"From who? *Me?*"

"Of course not." He glanced away.

Mason caught the truth loud and clear. His father still didn't want his son involved in Emma's life. "Then why did you ask me to come here when you could have gotten Darlene or another officer to watch over them?"

His dad plunked himself in the rocking chair and buried his face in his hands. "Because I don't trust anyone but you, son."

Mason sat on the couch, more emotions swarming in his head than he could handle right now. His undeniable attraction to Emma occupied his mind, but his father was right. He couldn't start anything. She was his brother's wife. Plus, the heartache he'd gone through with Zoe scarred him against ever getting involved with another woman again.

The broken grandfather clock before him jolted

Mason's resolution never to forgive the man. Was he also chipping at the ice around his heart?

"Dad, you need to remove the camera," he mumbled. "You've upset Emma."

His father glanced up. "I already did. It's gone." A pause. "I heard what you said about me. There's a reason I asked you to stay away from them."

"Tell me. Brady wouldn't have wanted that."

"I know you asked her on a date years ago, and I was concerned about you getting too close. I was just protecting my granddaughter."

Mason needed to change the subject before he said something he'd regret. Rolling his shoulders to extinguish the frustration that churned through him, he pulled out the marshal's business card and passed it over. "This is the name Skip wanted to give me as the mole before his untimely death."

His father took the card and peered at the name. "I've heard of Deputy Rollins. From what I understand, he's one of their best marshals in the western district of New York. It can't be him."

"Skip said he got the information from a reliable source, Dad."

"I'll look into it." He pointed to a box in the corner. "Tracey retrieved all of Emma's files. She also moved any electronic ones from her laptop to yours. Said someone could hack into the personal one too easily."

"Understood. Thanks for getting those." Mason rubbed the stubble on his chin. "There still has to be someone from our division leaking information, especially about Skip being my CI."

"I have no idea. I've vetted everyone personally."

"You don't think the mole is Darlene, do you?"

His father shot him a look. "How can you say that? She's your partner." He released a weary sigh. "I've been praying for insight into the situation."

Mason lifted a fluffy cushion and slouched back into the couch. "Praying, Dad? How will that help?"

"Why don't you believe? You did as a boy."

Mason squeezed the pillow. "That was before God stole everything from me, including your respect."

His father bolted from the rocking chair. "*What?* You think I don't respect you? That's absurd. What's really going on, Mason?"

Isabelle James's lifeless eyes flashed before him. A sight he couldn't wipe from his memory. "Nothing."

His father squeezed Mason's shoulder. "Son, you need to come back to God."

He must convince his father that would not happen. His hardened heart was too far gone. Besides, he doubted God would want his brokenness. Not after Mason had faulted Him for everything.

He stood. "It's time you left. I need to secure the farmhouse and check the perimeter before we all go to bed."

His father walked to the door and turned. "I am proud of you, son. Even if you don't believe it."

Mason would let the comment slide. "Dad, there's nothing going on between Emma and me. And there won't be. G'night."

His father looked like he had more to say on the matter, but he left without another word.

Mason locked the door behind him and turned. Emma stood at the end of the hall, a tear glistening.

"Em, I—"

"Don't. I know you're just going to run away again once we wrap up this case." She grabbed Jerome from a chair and marched back to the bedroom.

Mason leaned against the door and closed his eyes. His no-win plight zapped the energy from his body.

He had to rectify the situation. Quickly.

Emma shut the bedroom door and leaned against it, wiping the tear away before it rolled down her cheek. Determination set in over not wasting emotions on the man who'd just declared he wouldn't stick around in their lives. She'd been crazy to think or even wish he would.

Shrugging off any more notions of Mason, she walked to the bed and held out the giraffe. "Jerome wants to kiss you good-night." Emma made kissing noises and tapped the animal's nose in Sierra's face.

Her daughter giggled.

Emma's shoulders relaxed. The sound calmed her stormy emotions. She tucked Jerome beside her daughter and kissed her cheek. "Night, baby girl. I love you."

"Wuf you." Sierra's eyelids drooped closed. The excitement from the past couple of days had tuckered her daughter out, and Emma was thankful they had a safe place to lay their heads.

At least she prayed that was the case.

She turned on the night-light and snapped off the lamp. Her daughter did not do well in the dark.

Neither had Emma.

Ever since her husband had almost strangled her in the middle of the night, she'd slept with a light on to curb her fears. Brady had taken her by surprise, and she'd vowed she'd never sleep in total darkness again. She prayed God would remove the terror, but it remained. Emma fisted her hands at the memory. It was a bleak time in her life and one she'd never forget. She hadn't even told her sister, Holly, about Brady, and they were extremely close. Why she had kept it to herself, she didn't know. Perhaps the shame from not reading the man's ferocious side before she married him stood in her way.

Plus, Mason brought back too many memories

of Brady. They looked and sounded so much alike. Could she ever get past that?

A soft knock sounded. "Emma, can we talk?"

She had to face him sometime. Squaring her shoulders, she took in a huge breath and opened the door. "Let's go to the kitchen. I want to look at the box your dad brought."

Mason peeked around her to observe Sierra. "She's asleep already?"

"Yes, apparently all the puzzle building zapped her energy today." Emma closed the door and followed him to the outer living area.

"Do you want a tea?" Mason asked.

"Sure. Peppermint, please."

He filled the kettle and set it on the stove. Meanwhile, she gathered her research box and carried it to the kitchen table.

They both needed each other right now, so she knew she must approach the subject carefully to maintain a peaceful working relationship. He had to move on from his brother's death, and she required his protection.

"About what I said earlier—" he began.

"Mason, there's nothing more to say. I understand it's hard to be reminded of the loss of your brother, and Sierra and I don't help. I get it." She opened the box and pulled out file folders, notebooks and a stack of pictures.

Mason grabbed the tea tin. "Em, I'm not planning on running away this time. I know you heard what Dad and I said, but he can't keep me away any longer."

Their gaze locked.

The kettle hissed, breaking their moment.

Mason reached into the cupboard.

Emma picked up a folder and opened it. "I'm glad, Mason. Sierra needs you in her life, and I could use a friend."

His shoulders slumped, and he glanced back at her before removing two cups.

She caught a hint of emotion in his eyes. Disappointment? Relief?

Whatever it was, she had to concentrate on stopping the Luthers so she and Sierra could go home. Home to her family.

Not indulge in pointless romantic fantasies of something happening with Brady's brother.

"Okay, where do we start?" She sat and peered at the papers in the file. "Layla Luther. Forty. Never married. Engaged once, but she broke it off."

Mason placed her tea in front of her. "Here you go." He plopped down and opened his laptop. "Do you know why she ended things?"

"Not officially, but sources close to the family stated her fiancé humiliated her in public one time. That was all it took."

He typed on his laptop. "From what I've read, she sounds like the type of woman you don't want to cross."

"Not at all. She's ruthless but also very compassionate when it comes to Layla's Centre of Hope."

"The abuse centre for women. Do you think she was abused? Is that why she's so passionate about it?"

Emma dunked her tea bag up and down to strengthen it. "I've suspected that for a long time but could never prove it. Wasn't my job to. I helped the task force bring down her dad. That's all. Both Layla and Lance are squeaky clean."

"Border patrol confirmed Lance has not returned to New York yet. What type of business could he be doing here for his marketing firm?"

"Just a sec." Emma shuffled through folders until she found the one she'd marked "Lance" and opened it. "Okay. Luther Marketing Firm. Established ten years ago. They specialize in helping small businesses get word out about their organizations." She thumbed through the papers and stopped short. A rush of heat turned her hands clammy. "Are you thinking he's here to get to all the witnesses?"

"I don't know." He reached across the table and placed his hand over hers. "He will not get to you and Sierra. Dad and I have your backs."

Ignoring what his touch did to her insides, she pulled away and took a sip of tea. "Let's go over all these files and see if we can find anything new. You know what they say about fresh eyes, right?" She handed him a stack.

"I do." His lips turned upward into a captivating grin.

A smile she could get used to seeing every day. "Let's get to work."

Emma rubbed her eyes after poring through the files for two hours. She glanced at her watch. Ten o'clock. Her weary body required rest.

She pinched her lips together and resisted the urge to bang on the table. So far they had found nothing new.

Mason straightened. "Wait. What was the lawyer's name who drew up Layla's papers for her nonprofit organization?"

Emma sifted through the files until she found the information. "Will Gowland. Why?"

He held up a piece of paper. "He's not only the same lawyer that Lance used for his business, but he also worked behind the scenes on their father's trial. I thought the brother and sister were estranged from each other and their father. Why would they all use the same lawyer?"

Her jaw dropped. "I never connected that information. Hang on. I'm pretty sure I have a picture of him." She shuffled through the box. "Here he is." She held it up.

Mason peered closer. "I'll get Dad to look into it. Maybe he can contact the Buffalo PD and have someone interview Mr. Gowland."

"Good idea." She stood. "I need to go to bed."

"Of course. I'll—"

His cell phone buzzed and vibrated on the table. He read the screen, bolting out of his chair.

Emma's heartbeat skyrocketed. "What is it?"

"Text from Darlene. Your coworker, Heath Allen, was just found shot in his safe house."

"No!" She grabbed the sides of the chair.

Did Heath's death mean she was next?

Mason rushed to Emma's side and pulled her into his arms. Sobs shook her body, and he held tighter, caressing the back of her head. "It's gonna be okay, Em. They're unaware of our location." He hoped. Tightness assailed his chest. They needed answers, and fast.

He rested his chin on the top of her head. Her lavender shampoo wafted into his nose, and he inhaled. If it wasn't for the circumstance, he could get lost in her embrace.

Forever.

Her earlier comment about him being only a friend gnawed at him. What if he wanted more? Would Brady approve? They'd once joked how Emma had chosen him over Mason, but his brother had been gone for three years now.

No, Mason. You can't.

He released her and held her at arm's length. "I'm so sorry for your loss. Were you and Heath close?"

She nodded. "He was a great friend. I can't believe he's gone." She pounded on Mason's chest. "We need to stop whoever is doing this."

He grabbed her arms. "I know, and I will."

Emma backed away. "You can't promise that, Mason."

"I will do everything in my power to protect you and Sierra. With my life." He caressed her cheek. "That I *can* promise, Em."

"I need to call his brother, Jace. They were extremely close."

Mason sat. "That's not wise right now."

"I *have* to, Mason. Heath was the only family Jace had. He'll take the loss hard, and I want to tell him I'm praying for him."

He glanced her way. "How did you meet Jace?"

"Heath is…*was* originally from BC and transferred here once he became a border patrol agent. Jace is a police officer in British Columbia. He visited his brother twice a year. Heath tried to set us up shortly after Brady's death, but I wasn't ready. We became friends. Please let me do this. Your cell is safe, right?"

Someone could probably hack any device in today's age. Should he take the risk? "Fine." He passed his cell phone to her. "Keep the conversation brief."

She punched in a number and hit the speakerphone icon.

"Jace here," a deep voice said.

"It's Emma."

"Oh, hey. I'm surprised to hear from you. Aren't you also in WPP?"

Emma's jaw dropped. "How did—"

"I'm a cop, remember? Heath missed our weekly call, and after I learned about the Luther crime organization being taken down by a special task force, I put it all together."

"Right. You're on speaker with Constable James. He let me call you from his secure line. I'm so sorry about Heath. I know you were close."

"I can't believe he's gone." Jace's voice quivered before he cleared his throat. "Listen, Emma. You're an answer to prayer."

"How's that?" she asked.

"I had to get in touch with you and wasn't sure how. I just received an encrypted email from Heath five minutes ago."

Mason stiffened. "Are you sure it's from him?"

The other man let out a staggered breath. "Positive. He used a secret code we developed as kids."

Emma grabbed a pen and paper. "What did he say?"

"He said, 'Bro, if you're receiving this email, they got to me. I requested the cop protecting me send the message upon my death. I encrypted the contents as I don't trust anyone but you. I discovered evidence I couldn't share until now for fear of Lincoln's men coming after the entire team, and I wouldn't put their lives in jeopardy. However, it now seems the Luthers' tentacles reach far and wide. I'm attaching financial records of Luther Marketing Firm showing large cash payments to witnesses testifying against Lincoln Luther. This could help prove Lance was in cahoots with his dad even though he claimed innocence.'"

Mason caught Emma's pleased expression. "How did Heath get this information, Jace?"

"I'm guessing he hacked into their company," he said. "He was always good with computers. I know what you're thinking. It's inadmissible in court."

Emma's smile faded, and she dropped her pen. "Right. Anything else in the email?"

"No. Just a personal goodbye to me."

Mason heard the grief in the man's voice. "I'm sorry for your loss, Jace, and I hate to ask you this, but can you forward the information to us?" He gave him his email address.

"Of course. Emma, don't let my brother's death be in vain. Bring that family down."

"We will do everything in our power to do that," she promised.

"Please be safe."

Emma's lip trembled before tears streamed down her cheeks.

Mason grabbed her hand and squeezed. "I will see to it, Jace."

"Counting on you. 'Bye." He clicked off.

"You okay?" Mason rubbed her hand with his thumb.

She snatched it back. "I'm tired of this family getting away with everything."

"Agreed, but this additional information will make the authorities look closer into the Luther Marketing Firm." Mason's cell phone rang, and he glanced at the screen. "Dad."

"I need to go to bed," Emma said. "Please make sure the house is safe."

"I will. Sleep well."

"I doubt it, but I'll try." She walked down the hall.

He hit Answer on his phone. "Hey, Dad." An email notification sounded on his laptop. He put his father on speaker and opened the Excel attachment. Luther Marketing Firm's financials appeared.

"Mason, did you hear about Officer Allen?" His father's voice rang with urgency.

"Yes, Darlene texted me. We talked to his brother, Jace, a moment ago."

"What? How could you risk that?"

"Before you jump down my throat, let me tell you something interesting, Dad." Mason explained the call and told him about the spreadsheet. He forwarded the information to his father's email and shut his laptop. "Check into it and see what you can find."

"Will do. Listen, Forensics tested the insulin, and the results match Jeff's findings. The vial contained fentanyl."

"Not surprised." Mason moved to the window and parted the blinds. "Dad, are we secure here at the farmhouse?"

Two unmarked cruisers still sat outside. One in the driveway and one on the side of the highway. Mason glanced around. No signs of movement.

"I spoke to Constables Nash and Lucas. They did a sweep moments ago, and you're good. The grounds are nice and quiet."

"Any word if other witness locations were compromised?"

"I'm checking now. I'll also inquire about Deputy Rollins. Keep you posted."

"Wait…before you go." Mason closed the blinds. "Dad, can you look into a lawyer named Will Gowland? He seems to be a common denominator between all the Luthers."

"Will do. Stay safe, son. I'm praying." His father hung up.

For once, Mason was happy to have the prayers. He just hoped they'd help.

He walked to the door and checked the locks. Bolted. He ensured he set the alarm before heading to bed.

A loud thud followed by breaking glass woke him. He bolted upright. Had someone bypassed the constables? A quick glance at his watch told him it was 3:00 a.m. He had to get to Emma and Sierra. Before—

Crash!

His bedroom wall crumbled, and a chunk of drywall hit him. A glow of headlights shone through the dusty debris.

Someone had breached the house by plowing into it.

They had to escape. Pushing the wall piece aside, he jumped out of bed.

Stars danced in his vision and the room spun before he collapsed into total darkness.

SEVEN

Emma sat up in bed. Somehow she'd been in a deep sleep and a noise registered, but a second crash fully jarred her awake. She couldn't wait to discover the source of the bang, because something told her they needed to run. Again. She jumped out of bed and stuffed Jerome and her medical bag in a knapsack, securing it on her back. She lifted Sierra, blanket and all, and dashed from the room.

A cloud of dust filled the hallway, and she struggled to move forward in the pitch blackness. "Mason! *Mason!* Are you all right?" Her hushed, urgent whispers boomed in the corridor.

No response.

Sierra stirred in her arms. It wouldn't be long before her daughter woke and started screaming. She hated the dark.

The hall cleared slightly, and the outside streetlight illuminated the front living area. A reinforced truck had rammed into the house. The vehicle's large tires had demolished everything in its path.

Emma gulped as a question arose. Where was the driver? Knocked out from the collision? She didn't wait to find out and kept moving.

She reached Mason's door, only to find it demolished. "Mason." She stepped inside his room and found him on the floor, unconscious.

She squatted beside him and set Sierra down. She placed her fingers on his neck. Steady pulse. *Thank You, Lord.* She nudged him. "Wake up! Come on, Mason. We need you."

Movement sounded from the living room. Someone had breached the premises. She shook him harder. "Mason, we need to get out of here. They found us!"

He stirred and blinked open his eyes.

Emma leaned closer to whisper. "Mason, can you hear me?"

"Em? What happened?"

"Someone rammed their vehicle into the house." She glanced toward the obliterated wall.

A shadow passed in front of the glowing headlights.

Her pulse hastened, pounding in her head. "We need to get out of here. Now!"

Mason eased himself up and pointed. "Gun. Flashlight. Cell phone. Laptop. Nightstand." His raspy words divulged his condition.

Would a possible concussion inhibit their escape? She ignored the question and grabbed his belongings.

He shoved his shoes on barefooted. "I'll take Sierra. You know how to shoot, right?"

"Yes." She stuffed his laptop in the backpack and his cell phone in her pocket.

Mason lifted her daughter into his arms. "We'll go out the back. You cover us."

She sneaked from the room and raised the weapon but kept the flashlight off. No sense in announcing their location.

Someone shuffled through debris, heading in their direction. She turned to Mason. "Go!"

He rushed past her with Sierra, soundless.

Thank You, Lord, for keeping Sierra asleep.

Emma tiptoed down the hall and followed Mason out the back door.

He hesitated and glanced in every direction. Thankfully, the moon provided ample lighting to ensure no one was in the backyard and aided in their escape.

"I don't see anyone," he said. "We're going to run to the tree line. Don't stop for anything. You hear?"

She nodded and darted across the rough terrain, trying to regulate her breathing. Somewhere in the distance, a wolf howled. A shiver coursed through her. Not only did they have to deal with men and guns, but wildlife, too.

The tree line beckoned them forward. She uttered a quick prayer for safety and kept moving. Emma stumbled over a branch but caught her footing. *Almost there.* Adrenaline fueled her body, and she squashed the overwhelming sensation of dread creeping into her limbs. She couldn't stop now. Their lives depended on their escape.

Mason reached the woods and stopped behind a massive tree trunk.

She dropped beside him. "Do you think they saw us run?"

He peeked his head up. "I don't see anyone, but that means nothing. Give me my cell phone."

She pulled it from her pocket and handed him the device.

He punched a key and waited. "Dad, they found us!"

A mumbled reply sailed through the phone.

"We're in the woods just behind the farmhouse." A pause. *"Hurry."* He moved the phone away from his mouth. "He's looking for a place we can hide."

Sierra stirred in his grip. The blanket slipped, exposing her head. Emma tucked it in to protect her sweet baby girl.

A light bounced in the distance behind the farmhouse.

They were coming.

"Mason! We've got to run." She eased up but kept herself in a crouch-walk position.

"Go!" Mason pointed to deeper in the woods.

She ran, feeling her way through the bushes and hanging branches. The moonlight hid the full foliage, but she didn't want to turn on the flashlight.

"Dad, we're on the move. They've figured out we escaped. Are any of the constables alive out front? Can you call them and get them to create a diversion?" A pause. "Call me back."

"Mason, where can we hide?"

"Dad is still studying a map." He peered down at her daughter. "How is she not awake?"

"She loves movement. When she was a baby, I had to place her in the car seat and put her on the washer to get her to sleep sometimes."

"Good thing. Keep going. Turn the light on, but put your hand over it. That will conceal the glow but still give us a beam to follow." She obeyed and raced onward. Her chest constricted, and she wheezed. A branch slapped her in the face, and she nearly lost her footing again. Her weakened legs couldn't take much more. She stopped and leaned against a tree. "Can't. Go. On." Her breath came out in pants. *Lord, give me strength.*

Mason swayed before grabbing the tree trunk. "We have to, Em."

"Are *you* okay? You were unconscious when I found you."

"Little bump on the head. I'm fine."

She doubted his assessment. Emma glanced at Sierra. God closed her mouth like the lion in the book of Daniel. The question was, though, for how long?

Mason's phone buzzed. "What do you have, Dad?" He paused. "Where?" He waited for a few more seconds. "Okay, thanks." He clicked off.

"What is it?"

"Nash was knocked out but is still alive. He's taken up pursuit. Dad said we should reach a clearing any minute now and there's an abandoned barn at the other side. He's sending someone to pick us up."

"But who can we trust? How did they find us?" They were missing something. Somehow the suspects had stayed two steps ahead of them the entire time.

"Not sure. There were no trackers on our vehicle."

Shouts sounded from the other side of the trees. A shot boomed, echoing into the night.

A sudden breeze gathered strength, rustling the leaves.

"We need to keep moving," Mason told her.

Ten minutes later, they reached the edge of the woods. Emma shone the light over the area and stopped on their destination. She pointed. "There!"

A rickety, abandoned barn barely stood across the field.

Darkness hid its actual condition, but she suspected a strong wind would topple the building.

Their only source of protection was no salvation at all.

Even in the disappearing moonlight, Mason caught Emma's widened eyes and ashen complexion. Her alarmed face contorted at the sight of the place where they needed to take shelter.

The one place that could prove as dangerous as the men following them.

However, they had no choice but to seek refuge in this dilapidated barn.

Mason glanced at the fast-moving clouds. They now covered most of the stars, and only a small moonbeam shone.

Emma's disheveled red hair danced in the wind.

The weather had turned against them.

"We need to take shelter now," he said.

"This building is our only hiding place?"

Another muffled gunshot exploded beyond the tree line.

"It's the barn or the men behind us. Let's pray those shots didn't take out Nash and the assailants don't find us. We could be sitting ducks." He pointed at the barn. *"Run!"*

Heat lightning flashed in the distance. He tucked the blanket farther over Sierra's head and with Emma by his side kept running.

Within minutes, they reached the barn's entrance.

She shone the flashlight, exposing the building's condition. "I don't know, Mason."

The doors hung precariously from their hinges and thudded against the barn walls. Great. The noise would draw attention.

Emma moved the light's beam upward.

Missing shingles left rotted wood planks and holes splattered over the roof.

"Em, get inside."

She obeyed while he stood at the entrance.

Emma shone the light again, revealing a haystack against a half wall and a run-down, rusted tractor. A ramshackle set of wooden stairs led to a loft. No way would he take them up there.

Sierra stirred in his arms. "Do you have Jerome in case she wakes up?"

Emma took her backpack off and removed the giraffe.

"The signal says they're around here somewhere," one of the suspects said nearby.

Mason's heart pummeled his chest. *What signal?*

They had to hide. He pointed. "There, get behind the wall by the haystack."

Emma stumbled over a pitchfork, and Jerome flew into the air, landing in the entryway, just beyond Mason's reach. He did not have time to go back for the stuffed animal.

Lord, help Sierra stay asleep and conceal Jerome.

Would the Lord listen to his plea after Mason had ignored Him for so long?

He and Emma huddled behind the crumbling half wall. She shut the flashlight off and buried the device in her sweatshirt.

"Here, take Sierra and give me the gun," Mason whispered.

She passed the weapon to him.

He placed the sleeping four-year-old into Emma's arms. "Okay, stay as quiet as you can and pray Dad's constables get here fast."

Lightning flashed, illuminating the area.

Thunder rumbled. Wind shook the barn and the wobbly structure creaked in annoyance, waking Sierra.

She screeched, her wails enough to draw attention and expose their location.

Emma rocked her daughter. "Shh…baby girl. Stay quiet. Mama's got you."

"Over there!" a voice yelled. Footsteps pounded nearby and stopped. "Lookie here, a giraffe."

Mason peeked through a crack in the wall.

Another flash of lightning revealed two masked men raising rifles.

Mason lifted his gun, ready to fire.

Thunder boomed.

Sierra belted out another scream.

Emma clamped her hand over her daughter's mouth, but it didn't help. Her muffled cries revealed their hiding spot.

"Come out, come out, wherever you are," the voice mocked. "Of course we know where you are, Mason and Emma. That hay and broken-down wall won't shield you."

Mason couldn't wait. Protecting Emma and Sierra was his first priority.

"They want you all dead," another voice said.

Mason poked the barrel of his gun through a

hole in the wall and fired blindly in the direction of the man's voice.

One of the men cussed. "That was too close. I'm tired of this game of hide-and-seek. You're finished."

Approaching footsteps sounded. Mason peeked at the entrance. Lights bounced over the field like fireflies on a summer night.

Were they friend or foe?

"Police!" Constable Darlene Seymour yelled. "Give it up. You're surrounded."

Thank You, God.

The men fired toward Darlene's voice, and a shot whizzed above their heads.

Mason grabbed Emma and threw himself on top of her and Sierra. "Stay down."

He couldn't have any stray bullets hitting them.

More gunshots erupted.

One suspect moaned before a thud sounded.

"Barry. No!"

Silence.

"I surrender," the other man said.

Mason slowly eased himself up with his weapon trained and watched as Darlene shuffled into the building. "Let me see your hands," she demanded. The man set down his rifle, raised his hands and dropped to the dusty barn floor.

Another constable raced around him and cuffed his wrists.

Mason's partner checked Barry's pulse and called for an ambulance.

"Darlene, are they secure?" He wanted to be sure before bringing Emma and Sierra out of their hiding spot.

She shone her flashlight in their direction. "We're good. You can come out." She moved the beam. "Not sure if he'll live, though. His pulse is weak."

Mason helped Emma stand. Sierra's sobbing lessened. "You're safe now, Sisi." He rubbed the girl's tears away. "Uncle Mason loves you."

Emma's soft intake of breath drew his attention. Why had his words taken her by surprise? His absence from their lives hadn't meant he didn't care for his brother's family. However, his father's demand to keep him away should not have stopped Mason. He tightened his jaw. He would not avoid them this time around.

Even if it meant he and Emma could only be friends.

Sierra stopped crying and reached out to Mason.

He stuck his weapon in the back of his pants and lifted his niece. "I've got you."

She hiccuped.

The trio stepped out from behind the wall and haystack.

"Darlene, how did you get here so fast?" Mason asked.

Constable Nash stood over the suspect with his weapon trained. They were taking no risks.

"I was patrolling the area and heard your father's frantic call over the radio." She holstered her gun.

Something niggled in his brain. Why was she always in the right place at the right time?

Don't go there, Mason.

"Thank the Lord." Emma's words came out breathless. "Who knows what would have happened if you and the others weren't close by?"

"You got that right." Darlene hauled the prisoner to his feet and removed his mask. "Time to take you in."

"Wait." Mason handed Sierra back to Emma. "Can we at least ask a few questions here? I need answers."

"Of course." She cast her flashlight around the barn and stopped at a discarded metal chair. "Constable Nash, can you grab that chair?"

The officer holstered his gun and complied.

"Nash, we heard gunfire at the farmhouse. What happened?" Mason asked.

"Darlene called Tom away about fifteen minutes before the crash."

Mason turned to his partner. "Why did you do that? You knew we required two officers guarding the house."

"I needed his assistance with something, and we were short-staffed. I figured you'd be okay."

Heat rushed Mason, and he struggled to keep his emotions intact. His father would find out about Darlene's incompetence. Further skepticism prickled the back of his neck, trust for this woman dissipating.

He turned to Nash. "Go on."

"It all happened so fast. I heard tires screeching just before the truck barreled across the grounds and rammed into the front of the house. I ran from my vehicle but didn't see the other assailant. He got the drop on me and knocked me out." He rubbed the back of his head. "I woke up a few minutes later to see movement in the house. That's when I called for reinforcements and pursued them." He gestured toward other officers standing guard at the barn's entrance.

"Glad you're okay." Mason shoved the prisoner into the chair. "Tell me your name."

"Felix Carson." The man's gaze turned to the body on the barn floor. "That's Barry Ingle."

"Who hired you?" Mason split his stance.

"Someone posted a reward on the dark web."

"Who put it out?" Darlene asked.

"Someone within the Luther organization."

Emma stepped forward. "Which Luther?"

"Didn't say. The handle only said Luther Shipping."

Goose bumps electrified Mason's arms as distrust crept up his spine. Why would the company be so blatant and use their name? It made little sense. Had Lincoln ordered the hit from his prison cell?

"Did they include all witnesses?" He had to know if they were targeting everyone or just Emma.

The suspect glanced at Emma. "The hit only named her and you."

Her eyes bulged and she choked in a breath. "How did you find us?"

Felix eyed the giraffe.

Mason braced his arms at his side.

Someone had put a tracker in Jerome.

The fact they could get so close sent tremors coursing through his body.

EIGHT

Emma teetered, her jellied legs threatening to buckle. The extent of the Luthers' heinous plan suddenly became more real than it had in the past few weeks. They were intent on targeting both her and Sierra. Jerome was never far from her daughter. Questions plagued Emma's mind as to how they got to the giraffe.

She tightened her grip on Sierra. "Mason, we need to get out of here."

The little girl pointed. "I want Jerome."

Emma snapped her gaze to Mason. He knew how much Sierra relied on the stuffed animal. She prayed he would relent and allow her to have the toy.

Mason nodded and turned to Constable Nash. "Do you have a pocketknife?"

The officer pulled the multitool from a pocket and handed it to him.

Mason picked up Jerome and felt around its legs.

Darlene stepped closer to her partner. "What are you doing, Mason? That's evidence."

His eyes flashed an emotion Emma found hard to read. Annoyance? Mistrust? Clearly, his partner's earlier actions had him riled.

"My only concern right now is this little girl

and her mother, Constable. Sierra needs Jerome to feel safe."

His words thawed Emma's earlier resolve to remain just friends. The man before her cared deeply and sent butterflies dancing in her tummy. She squashed them. Now wasn't the time to go there.

Mason continued to inspect the giraffe and stopped at its right leg. "Got it." He cut a hole. "Hand me gloves, Nash. The tracker seems fairly large, so we may get prints off the device."

Constable Nash removed a pair from the pouch on his weapon belt and gave them to Mason.

Mason put them on and pulled out the rectangular device. He handed the giraffe to Sierra.

Her daughter's lip quivered. "Hole, Y'ncle Mason."

"Sorry, Sisi."

Emma kissed Sierra's forehead. "Don't worry, baby girl. We'll fix Jerome later."

Darlene held an evidence bag open. "I'll take the tracker."

Mason hesitated.

The undercover constable's reluctance to hand the gadget over to Darlene confirmed his suspicion of his partner.

Darlene tilted her head. "Mason, I will give it to Forensics."

He relented and dropped the tracker into the bag. "I'll call Dad to put a rush on the results."

His partner's shoulders slumped. "Why don't you trust me?"

"Let's not talk about this now. I need to get Emma to another safe house. I'm calling Dad." He pulled out his cell phone.

Darlene hauled Felix from the chair. "Time to finish our conversation at the station."

"Can you keep us updated?" Emma asked.

The woman glanced at Mason talking on his phone and groaned.

Emma squeezed Darlene's arm. "I'm sorry. He's under mega pressure."

"I understand, but it's just hard to see the suspicion in his eyes. Emma, I'm not the mole."

She prayed Darlene spoke the truth. A memory niggled through her mind but slipped beyond her reach. Something told her it was important to their case. Emma pounded her leg. *Why can't I remember?*

The constable escorted Felix from the barn.

Mason returned and pocketed his phone. "Okay, Dad is moving us to a safe house off the Niagara Parkway. Not on the main road, but farther into the countryside. He's sending the team to secure the location."

"Can we return to the farmhouse and get all my files?" Emma asked.

"The Luthers know you were there. We can't risk it."

All that research now lost. "Can't you ask a con-

stable to get the box? There's still something I need
to show you."

"What?"

"Pictures. I just remembered I didn't show them
all to you. A couple in particular."

"I'll call Dad on the way." Mason turned to Constable Nash. "Can we take your unmarked vehicle?"

The constable handed over the keys. "Of course."

Three hours later, after driving around to ensure they weren't being followed, Mason pulled
into the driveway of a modern bungalow. They had
debriefed the constables on the incident, and the
paramedics checked them for injuries before giving them the all clear. Unfortunately, Barry suc-
cumbed to the gunshot wound. Not that he knew
more information than his partner.

Emma stared at the house. The home sat on the
edge of a wooded area and included a tire swing
in the front yard. She pointed. "Sierra, look."

Sierra squealed. "Let's go swing, Mama!"

Emma's hand flew to her chest. Her daughter's
vocabulary was improving. She glanced at Mason.

He smiled.

Her heart hitched. Was his influence in her life
rubbing off on Sierra?

"Mama, swing?"

Sierra brought her back to the moment. "Mason,
are the grounds safe?"

"Let me check with Dad." Mason killed the engine. "Wait here." He stepped outside the car and pulled out his cell phone.

"Uncle Mason will be right back and then we can swing for a few minutes, but then you're gonna have a nap, okay, baby girl?" Emma needed her daughter to settle so she could also catch some sleep. Being interrupted in the middle of the night deprived her of the much-needed rest that her weary body craved.

Her daughter clapped. "Yay!"

Five minutes later, Mason opened the door. "Let's go swing, Sisi."

Emma and Sierra exited the car.

The little girl skipped to the tree.

Emma chuckled. "What did your dad say?"

He rubbed his brows with his thumb and index fingers. "The team is here and did a perimeter sweep. We're secure. Tracey also picked up your box. Apparently, some files were strewn about, as if someone riffled through them, so she's not sure if everything is there."

"Hopefully."

"Y'ncle Mason. *Now!*"

Mason chuckled. "Well, someone is impatient." He approached Sierra, lifted her and twirled her around.

She squealed.

A sound Emma loved.

After Mason pushed the four-year-old on the

tire for a few minutes, the trio walked inside the bungalow.

Tracey greeted them. "Welcome to your new home."

Emma prayed the woman spoke the truth. Sierra couldn't take much more running. *Neither can I.*

"Everything good, Tracey?" Mason asked.

"Yes. Alarm's installed and kitchen is stocked."

Emma walked into the living room. "No cameras this time?"

"No. Your father was adamant about that one. So sorry. I hated the fact he wanted to spy on you."

Mason followed behind Emma. "Not your fault. You were just doing your job."

"For what it's worth. He only wanted to keep his granddaughter safe."

She threw her hands up. "I get that, but it's still an invasion of privacy." Emma had always been a private person...and she had been through the wringer because of Brady's obsession. The thought of Seth James watching them ruffled her feathers. Yes, he was her father-in-law, but still. Her head pounded, and she felt her blood pressure rising.

Calm down.

She had to change the subject. "Did you bring puzzles?"

"Of course, and a sewing kit to fix Jerome." Tracey removed her glasses and shoved them into her front pocket. "He wanted to make sure you could fix the giraffe, so he asked for a kit. It's in the medicine cabinet along with all your other necessities." She turned to Mason. "I've restocked both of your clothes."

He held out his hand. "You're good at your job."

She returned the gesture. "I aim to please." A car pulled into the driveway. Tracey peered out the window. "Gotta run. Constable Lucas has arrived. Stay safe." She exited the house.

"Wow. Your dad thought of everything," Emma said.

"He's good at what he does, especially when it involves his Tiddlywinks." Mason winked.

"That's true."

He swayed and reached for the wall. "How about a quick breakfast?"

"Sure. Then I think everyone here needs a rest." She stepped forward. "You okay?"

He grabbed her hand. "I'm fine, Em. I'm more concerned about you gals."

His eyes softened with compassion, and her pulse quickened.

"We're good. I'm glad you're here."

Mason tucked one of her stray hairs behind her ear. "Me, too," he whispered.

Their eyes held.

Sierra edged herself between them and hugged Emma's legs. "Hungry, Mama."

Mason laughed and stepped backward. "Breakfast coming up."

Emma lifted her daughter and followed him.

But then she eyed the file box on the kitchen table, lurching her back into their predicament.

They had to solve the case in order for her and Sierra to get back to normalcy.

But did Emma now want an ordinary life without Mason?

The question bounced around her head. The answer sent jitters through her girded heart.

Mason's cell phone buzzed, jarring him awake. He bolted upward, and his stiff muscles screamed at him. He'd fallen asleep in the uncomfortable rocking chair reading one of Emma's files. Mason rubbed his neck and glanced at the screen. His father.

"Hey, Dad. You have an update?" His groggy voice exposed his sleep stupor, and he cleared his throat.

"Sorry to wake you, but I wanted to let you know we didn't get anything more from Felix. However, we had a hit on the prints from the tracking device."

Mason stood and peered out the window. Constable Lucas walked around the property line. "That was fast."

"Helps when you have connections."

"Well, was it one of the suspects we caught? The Luthers?"

"No. Deputy Darryl Rollins."

Mason fumbled with the phone. "The marshal

is the leak?" It made sense. He'd have access to their witnesses, but how did he get access to their files and locations?

"Let's not jump to conclusions. There's nothing else linking him."

"What about the business card Skip had in his pocket?" The thought of a fellow law enforcement officer leaking information to criminals steeled his jaw. Perhaps the Luthers' money enticed the man to betray his badge.

"Proves nothing."

Mason sat at the kitchen table and fingered a bag of cookies. "Has anyone interrogated him yet?"

"My contact in the Buffalo PD is trying to locate him. Nothing so far."

If Rollins had gone rogue, he would stay off the grid.

"How are Emma and Tiddlywinks?" The man's tone softened.

"Resting right now. Sierra loves the tire swing."

His father chuckled. "I figured she would. She'll also enjoy the pool out back. The shed is loaded with water wings. Okay, I have a meeting. Anything else?"

"Yes. Did you find out anything from Luther Marketing Firm's financial statements?"

"Only that there were suspicious withdrawals around the trial date. The transactions were encrypted, and with the verdict rendered and how the statements were obtained, I doubt the judge will reopen the case."

"Figures. Another question. Are you sure about Darlene?"

"Why do you doubt her, son?"

Mason strangled his grip on the table's edge, his emotions rising. "She pulled one constable off our detail. Why would she do that?"

"We've been short-staffed lately after recent cuts. She told me she required extra help, so I okayed it."

Wait—what? His father sanctioned removal of protection off his granddaughter? Mason tightened his grip on his cell phone. "Dad, why would you do that?"

"She required his help to investigate the truck that rammed the farmhouse."

"What did she find?"

"I was getting to that news." The chief superintendent rustled papers. "The truck had New York plates, and get this...the vehicle is owned by Layla's Centre of Hope."

Mason jumped up from the chair. "Seriously? Well, that puts both Lance and Layla on our radar."

"It does, but why would she use a truck that would be easily tied back to her organization? Makes little sense."

"That's a question I intend to ask. What's her number?" Mason grabbed a pen and paper, sitting back down.

More rustling came through the phone. "Got it." His father read the New York number to him. "Son, back to Darlene. She's never given me any indication of misplaced loyalties. She also saved your life once, remember?"

The image of Darlene's CI pulling a gun on Mason filled his vision. The man had accused Mason of betraying his confidence and was about to pull the trigger when his partner shot him. His father was right. The woman had saved him, so why couldn't Mason set aside the skepticism plaguing him?

"You're right." He would let it slide. For now.

"Talk later."

"Was that your dad?" Emma asked.

Mason had missed her approach.

She stood at the kitchen entrance, wiping her sleepy eyes. She'd changed into a green plaid shirt and leggings, but her messy hair caught his attention.

Was this totally adorable look the one Brady had encountered every morning during their marriage?

I want that, too.

The thought had taken over his mind before he realized it, but he now knew his feelings for this woman had grown in the past three days. If that was even possible.

"Mason?"

Get it together. She's off-limits, remember. Friends only.

"Take a seat. I have lots to tell you. First, I'll make some tea." He got up and walked to the stove, giving her the abridged version of his dad's conversation. "He also said they identified the fingerprint. Deputy Darryl Rollins."

Emma plopped down into a chair. "What? No way! He's so kind."

"You've met?"

"Yes, once, when I attended a joint US and Canadian law enforcement seminar. We chatted after he spoke on self-defense. He seemed very dedicated to his job. I doubt he'd betray a witness."

"Well, the Buffalo PD is looking for him. He has some explaining to do on why his print was on the tracking device placed in Jerome." Mason threw a tea bag in both their cups.

"Have you tried calling him from the card Skip had in his pocket?"

"Later. Right now I want to see the picture you were referring to earlier."

She walked to the box and carried it to the table. She rummaged through the contents and pulled out a couple of files. "I also remembered something else I had that might help in our investigation."

"Really? That's great." He shot her a curious look. "By the way, how did you get all this information? I didn't think that was part of a border patrol officer's role."

"Well, I did all this in my spare time. Didn't I

tell you I was the librarian in my high school and had a knack for sleuthing?"

He poured boiling water into their cups and brought them to the table. "You should ask Dad for a job."

"Right. *Not.*" She thumbed through some photos and pushed one across the oak surface. "Check this out."

He picked up the picture. His mouth dropped.

It was a shot of the Luthers standing beside Darlene at a benefit dinner.

"When was this taken?"

"There should be a time stamp on the back."

He turned the photo over. "Six months ago. Why didn't Darlene mention she knew the Luthers?"

"When Darlene showed up at the first safe house, I thought I'd seen her before but couldn't remember where. I hadn't looked at these files for months, and I never met your partner until recently. On the way back from the barn, a memory of seeing this picture dawned on me. I had to show you."

Mason dunked his tea bag up and down to quell the anger bubbling inside him. His earlier suspicions resurfaced. "What dinner was this?"

"A fundraiser for Layla's Centre of Hope in Buffalo."

"Why would Darlene attend?"

"No idea." Emma took a sip of her tea. "What other news did your dad have?"

"This is interesting. The truck that rammed the house is registered to Layla's organization."

She fumbled with her cup, tea spilling over the edge. "Why would she be so obvious by using one of her vehicles?" She grabbed a nearby tissue and dabbed at the liquid.

Mason set his phone in front of them. "Exactly what I'm going to ask her. Dad gave me the number to her organization. I'm hoping she's in the office."

"You're going to call? Won't you blow your cover?"

"I'm afraid that ship has already sailed. Promise me you'll stay quiet? I'll put the call on speaker, but she can't know you're with me. Understood?"

Emma nodded.

Mason punched in the number and waited.

"Layla's Centre of Hope. How may I direct your call?" the female asked.

"Layla Luther, please," Mason said. "Canadian police constable Mason James calling."

The receptionist put him on hold.

"Constable James, this is Layla Luther. How can I help you?"

He'd spare small talk and cut to the point. "Miss Luther, can you explain why a truck registered to Layla's Centre of Hope purposely rammed into a home here in Canada?" Hopefully, the element of surprise would trip her up.

"What? I have no idea. I can assure you, we only

use our trucks to help my girls. I can look into this, but first, what is the plate number?"

Mason rambled it off.

The sound of fingernails clicking on a keyboard muffled through the phone. He envisioned her manicured, bold-colored nails flying across her laptop. Nothing but the best for the woman.

"Here it is. Just as I suspected. That truck was stolen five days ago, which I reported to the police. You can verify that with the Buffalo PD."

"Can you tell me why your father is targeting the joint task force that sent him to prison? Or is it you and your brother?"

Emma opened her mouth but shut it quickly.

Mason imagined the question she wanted to ask. He held his index finger to his lips. He couldn't let her give away her presence.

"Mr. James, I can assure you none of my family is targeting anyone." The woman's pitch raised. "Dad is in prison. Lance and I are selling Luther Shipping to end any further speculation of his company being used for illegal activity. If you want to blame anyone, look closer at your own police force, namely your partner. Good day." She ended the call.

"She's referring to Darlene," Emma said. "How could she even know your partner's identity?"

"A question for Darlene when I get in touch with her." Mason pocketed his cell phone. "One thing's for sure. We hit a nerve. Did you hear her tone go up after I asked about her family?"

"I did. My spidey senses are telling me she's hiding something."

"Your *what* now?"

"Mama!" Sierra shuffled around the corner, dangling Jerome and interrupting their conversation. "Swing time."

"So much for finishing my tea." Emma took another sip and stood. "We won't be long."

"Take your time. Constable Lucas is outside. I'll see if I can determine why Darlene was at the fundraiser and talk to her about Layla. I'll also try calling Deputy Rollins."

She nodded and followed a bouncing Sierra out the front door.

Seemed the four-year-old had caught her second wind. Mason rubbed his sore neck muscles.

If only he could, too.

Emma pushed the tire swing and waited for Sierra's squeal. Each one got louder and louder. Emma's earlier trepidation faded with each scream. Her daughter was the only light in this darkened storm.

"Higher, Mama!"

"Baby girl, this is high enough."

A car pulled into the long driveway, sending the angst back into her body. She stopped the swing and grabbed Sierra. How had they gotten by Constable Lucas?

She squinted at the familiar vehicle and expelled a breath of relief. Tracey.

The computer tech exited her car.

"Did you forget something?" Emma asked.

Tracey shook her head. "I need to talk to you."

"About?"

"Your father."

Emma sucked in a breath. Something must have happened. Doctors had diagnosed her dad with stage-four pancreatic cancer, and Emma wasn't even able to say goodbye when she entered the WPP.

She picked the stuffed giraffe off the grass and handed it to Sierra. "Can you take Jerome over to the veranda and play with him for a minute?"

"Yes, Mama! Swing after?"

"O-of course."

Sierra ran to the wraparound veranda and sat on a rocking chair. Emma turned back to Tracey. "Is Dad okay?" She fingered her pendant and swallowed the lump forming in her throat.

"I'm afraid not. You told me about him when you first entered WPP, so I monitored your sister's social media accounts. She just posted asking for prayer, as they've moved him to palliative care. I figured you'd want to know."

Tears pooled. Her father was dying, and she

wasn't able to say goodbye or comfort her mother or sister. *Lord, what are You doing?*

Emma couldn't believe He allowed her dad's condition to worsen at a time when she had to stay hidden.

"How long does he have?" She held her breath, waiting for the answer she'd hate.

"Any day." She pulled out a phone and handed it to Emma. "You can't leave the safe house, but I brought you a burner phone. This goes against all the rules, and I could get fired. However, if I was in your shoes, I'd at least want to say goodbye. Do not tell them where you are. Don't talk long, and once you're done, destroy the phone. Just in case."

She threw her arms around Tracey. "Thank you."

"You're welcome." The tech returned to her car and drove away.

Emma glanced at her daughter to ensure Sierra was preoccupied before dialing her sister's cell number.

"Hello."

She sobbed and fell to the ground. How she had longed to hear Holly's voice.

"Emma? Is that you?"

"Yes."

Holly called for her mother to come to the phone. "I'm putting you on speaker. Where are you?"

"I can't tell you."

"Why, sweetheart?" her mother asked.

"I can't tell you that, either. It's so good to hear your voices. I miss you both."

"Ditto," Holly said.

"I found out Dad doesn't have long." Her voice quivered.

Her mother's sobs sounded through the phone.

"He doesn't, Emma. We don't…" Her sister's words faded.

She moved a stray curl behind her ear and wiped tears from her cheeks. "I can't talk long. Can you put the phone close to Dad's ear? I need—" She choked on her words. The thought of doing this over the phone tore at her heart. "I have to say goodbye."

Rustling buzzed through the airways.

"Okay, go ahead," Holly whispered.

"Hi, Papa. I miss you."

His heavy, sporadic breathing piped through the phone.

Emma covered her mouth to squash the cries she wanted to expel. "Papa, I will see you again one day where there will be no more pain. No more tears. We can go hunting for hazelnuts like we used to. I promise I won't step on a hornet's nest this time."

He moaned, or was it a laugh?

"I won't say goodbye, but see you later. I love you." Tears cascaded like a waterfall.

"Honey, when will you be able to come home?" her mother asked.

"I don't know, Mama." Emma stood and turned to check on Sierra.

But her daughter was nowhere to be found.

Mason punched in Darlene's number. No answer. He left a message and called his dad. Again, no answer.

Where were they? They both always had their phones nearby. He resisted the urge to pound the table.

Next, he dialed Deputy Rollins's number. Would he strike out three times? He slouched in the chair.

"Deputy Rollins here."

Finally. "This is Canadian police constable Mason James. I would prefer to talk to you in person, but I can't leave my witness. Are you available to come to Canada?"

"What's this about, Constable James?"

Mason stood and moved into the bedroom. "I've been working with Skip Perry. Can you tell me why he had your card in his pocket?"

"No idea. Never heard of the man."

"Right before he was shot, he was about to give me information regarding the Luther crime family and a mole in the US Marshals. Then I found your card. Can you explain?"

"I can assure you the mole is not me," Deputy Rollins told him. "I was almost shot protecting a witness from the Buffalo PD department."

"Why are your fingerprints on a tracking device used to locate our safe house?"

"Someone within the Buffalo PD asked me the same question." He paused. "Not sure."

His hesitation suggested to Mason the man held information back.

A ding sounded through the phone.

"Just a second, Constable. I have my laptop set up to get alerts on any Luther activity on the dark web."

Mason heard typing. "What's going on, Deputy?"

The man spewed a few not-so-nice words.

"I've just been notified someone within the Luther organization put out a million-dollar reward for the execution of our witnesses and lists their locations. A raid on all safe houses. Today."

"What?" Mason raced out of the bedroom. "I gotta go." He clicked off.

He barreled through the front doors. "Emma!"

She stood with her hands on top of her head, a twisted look on her face.

"What happened?" Mason held his breath.

Emma hurled a cell phone against the bungalow's brick siding. The device shattered. "I can't find Sierra. She's gone. My baby girl's gone and it's all my fault."

No! Mason had heard the sweet sound of Sierra's laughter a few minutes ago. He shouldn't have left them alone. What kind of protector was he?

Years of incompetency ingrained to him by his father roiled through him. Would he ever be able to prove he was worthy?

Lord, don't do this. Mason couldn't lose the little girl he now loved like a daughter.

NINE

Vertigo attacked Emma with the force of a charging elephant. She dropped to the veranda's wooden deck and sobbed. She had to enter the WPP, her father was dying and now Sierra was missing. *God, why aren't You listening?* She covered her face with her hands, willing the spinning to stop.

Mason wrapped his arms around her. "What happened?"

She pushed away and stood, waiting for her body to stay balanced. "We need to find her." Emma ran and shouted Sierra's name until her voice cracked. Then she moved around the side of the house and stopped in her tracks.

A fenced pool caught her attention and sent tremors throughout her body. An image of her at six years old flailing in her friend's pool flashed through her mind—the age her fear of water began. Her parents sent her for counseling, but she was never able to totally eliminate the hounding fear of drowning. What if—

No! She sprinted over to the fence and whipped open the gate, terrified at what she would find.

Nothing.

She punched out a breath, relieved her daughter hadn't entered through the gate.

Emma backed out and closed the door. Turning around, she spied the tree house and imagined her daughter climbing the ladder. She headed toward the perfect spot for her daughter to play hide-and-seek.

"Wait!" Mason yelled.

Pounding footsteps told her he followed.

"Constable Lucas, we need help," Mason said. "Sierra is missing, and I just found out there's a hit out on all safe houses. Call for reinforcements."

Emma stopped and whirled toward him. "What did you say?"

He told her about the hit.

A new wave of terror ricocheted through her. The Luthers had found her location, and now her daughter would pay the price. Emma hurried up the tree house's ladder. Maybe Sierra was only playing, but then again, why hadn't she answered when Emma yelled her name? She reached the top and knew what she'd find in the wooden playhouse.

Nothing.

Emma turned back around, and something caught her eye at the tree line.

Jerome.

She pointed. "Over there!" She scrambled down the ladder. "Sierra!"

The duo hurried to the edge of the woods and stopped at the sound of muffled voices.

Mason pulled her back and motioned for her to

be quiet. He pulled out his weapon and moved in front of Emma. "Stay behind me," he whispered.

They hunched low and walked into the woods, stepping lightly in stealth mode.

"Come on, little girl," a voice said. "I have some candy for you just through the woods."

Emma clamped her hand over her mouth to silence the fear. Sierra was in danger, and they had to save her. *Lord, I'm sorry for yelling at You. Please keep my baby girl safe.*

They moved closer and hid behind a massive oak tree.

"Want Jerome," Sierra said.

Emma caught a flash of her daughter's red curls.

"This is Pia the Pig. Don't you like her?" the voice asked.

"No!" Sierra swatted the animal to the ground.

"That's it. I've had enough, spoiled brat."

Sierra yelled. "Mommy!"

Emma couldn't wait any longer. She pushed past Mason. "Let my daughter go!"

The woman snapped her head in Emma's direction. Her hoodie slipped off, revealing her spiked blond hair.

Mason rushed to Emma's side, his weapon raised. "Give it up. You're surrounded."

The spindly woman's eyes bulged. She tightened her grip around Sierra, removed a gun from her pocket and held the weapon to the four-year-old's head. "Stay back. Or. Else."

Sierra whimpered within her captor's hold.

"It's okay, baby girl. Mama's here." Emma held out her hands and inched forward. "Let. Her. Go."

"Or what? Your boyfriend will shoot me?"

Mason moved closer. "You harm one hair on that little girl's head and I won't hesitate." He raised his weapon higher.

Footsteps alerted them to others approaching. Help had arrived.

The woman turned in the direction of the noise.

"Give it up, lady," Mason said. "Let Sierra go."

Constable Lucas crept behind her from another direction and pressed his nine-millimeter into her back. "Drop the weapon! You have nowhere to run."

The woman let go of the gun and Sierra simultaneously.

Constable Lucas kicked the Glock out of her reach.

Emma squatted and held out her arms. "Here, baby girl."

"Mama." Sierra raced into Emma's hold.

She stood and lifted her daughter into her tight embrace.

Mason tousled Sierra's curls and kissed her forehead. "So glad you're okay, Sisi." He turned to the woman. "Who hired you to abduct this child?"

"I ain't talkin' to you." She chomped on her gum.

Constable Lucas holstered his weapon and pulled

her arms behind her, cuffing the woman. "If you realize what's good for you, you will answer the question."

"I want a lawyer."

Emma took a step toward her. "How dare you scare my child! Did the Luthers hire you?"

She clamped her lips closed.

Mason stuffed his gun in the back of his pants and picked up the woman's weapon. "Are you even aware who you almost abducted? This little girl's grandfather is a powerful man. You will have the wrath of him and the entire police force come down on you if you don't tell us."

Her eyes widened.

Seemed the police threat scared the woman after all.

"I—I don't have a name. The dark web only provided the location and the little girl's description, stating the reward."

"What's your name?" Mason demanded.

"Evie." The woman chewed her lip. Her earlier tough demeanor disappeared.

"What were your drop-off instructions?" Constable Lucas asked.

"To take her to a park unharmed." She named the location. "Then I'd get my money. But I swear, I don't know who put out the hit."

Emma shifted the whimpering Sierra in her arms. "What time?"

"An hour from now."

Emma glanced at Mason.

He rubbed his brow using his thumb and index fingers. A motion she now thought of as his thinking pose.

"Mason, what are you planning?" she asked.

"Constable, take Evie to the station and see if you can get anything else from her." Mason guided Emma back through the woods. "We need to keep that meet up. It could help us find out who's behind everything."

"Why didn't you tell Constable Lucas?"

He stopped. "I'm not sure who I can trust. How did this woman get by him?"

"Okay, I get it. But I can help. I can pretend to hold a child under a large coat with a hoodie. Like Evie's."

"You will do no such thing."

Emma had to explain her need to be useful in this case. "Mason, I let my guard down. This was my fault. I need to rectify the situation."

"What do you mean?"

She explained to him about Tracey's visit and her talking on the phone to her father. "I'm sorry. Yes, calling was reckless, but how could I not say goodbye?" Her voice quivered.

He gathered her and Sierra into his arms.

A place she'd now love to stay.

"You're not who I blame. Tracey knows better."

Emma pulled back. "Don't get her in trouble. She was only trying to help."

"What if the phone had a tracking device?"

"There wasn't. She told me to destroy it."

Mason averted his gaze. "I understand you wanted to talk to your father, but this is your and Sierra's lives, Em. Any contact could not only put you at risk, but your family, too." His cell buzzed. "That's Dad. He's probably caught wind of this and will move us."

"Again?"

"Yes, we're no longer safe here."

"At least tell him the plan to keep the meet up."

He nodded then walked away to take the call.

Leaving Emma holding her trembling daughter.

Thank You, Lord, for saving Sierra. Help us solve this case.

Mason sat on a park bench an hour later with a ball cap pulled low on his forehead and guarded Emma with eagle eyes. His father had agreed to the nutty plan to put Emma in harm's way. Mason didn't like it, but she had walked over to where he'd been talking to his father and grabbed the phone, convincing Seth to allow her to do this. Mason had insisted Darlene go in her place, but the constable was nowhere to be found. That further raised his suspicions about her, but he'd set aside thoughts of Darlene for now. He needed to concentrate on the beautiful woman across the pathway.

Because, unfortunately, Emma was their only option on such short notice.

Mason had only agreed to the plan if they armed and wired her. His father agreed.

Seth had safely tucked Sierra away in a location not even they knew about. The plan was to grab whoever set up the drop-off and interrogate them.

Emma slouched on a bench with a doll stuffed under the bulky hoodie jacket hiding her red hair and a Glock jammed into her jeans. His father had told her to keep the weapon for protection. She'd reassured Mason the CBSA trained them well in defensive tactics and she could handle herself. Then made a point of reminding him that she hadn't gotten this far in her career by sitting on the sidelines. While he didn't doubt her abilities, especially in protecting her daughter, he was only concerned with keeping the woman he'd come to care about safe.

Concentrate on the task at hand.

Mason shifted his sunglasses and turned the page of the newspaper he'd been holding to keep up appearances. Nothing could go wrong on this sting operation. There was too much at stake.

He checked his watch. The suspect was late.

Mason crunched the sides of the paper, tightening his grip. *Why did you agree to this, Dad?*

A woman approached, pushing a stroller, and silenced his thoughts. His adrenaline spiked as she advanced closer.

A male jogger came from the opposite direction. He, too, had a ball cap and glasses on.

Were they looking for a man or a woman?

Mason couldn't get an unobstructed view of either.

He folded the newspaper, pretending to read the reverse side as he reached around and gripped his Smith & Wesson stuck in the waistband of his cargo pants.

A group of ravens shrilled in the trees above him, sending chills throughout his body. Seemed the birds sensed the pending danger and were warning them to be on guard.

Mason shifted in the seat and eyed Emma.

Apparently she, too, spotted the man and woman. She spoke to the doll in a hushed tone, playing her role flawlessly.

Smart. Emma knew what she was doing. She pulled the hood farther down on her head.

The man stopped short of the bench and knelt to tie his sneaker.

The woman kept walking.

Which told Mason the man was their target. The guy mumbled something in Emma's direction.

She lifted her gaze slightly. "She's right here." Emma adjusted the doll's hat to reveal red hair.

The man moved closer. "Why is she so quiet?"

"I drugged her to keep her calm."

He moved closer and pulled out an envelope. "Your payment. Now, I'll take her."

Emma shifted her gaze to Mason. "Isn't it a beautiful day?"

Their catchphrase for him to move in.

Mason threw the newspaper down and whipped out his weapon, sprinting across the pathway. "Stop! Police!"

Emma dropped the doll and pulled her Glock. "Give it up."

The man swore and turned to run.

Mason tackled him like a linebacker on a football field. He thrust his knee in the man's spine and pulled his hands back, cuffing him. Then he hauled him to his feet and shoved him onto the bench.

Emma kept her weapon trained on him.

Exhaling a harsh breath, Mason snatched the man's hat off to see his face and stilled.

Will Gowland—the Luthers' lawyer.

"We know who you are," Mason said. "Which Luther hired you to grab Sierra?"

"I know my rights. I'm not talking."

"Do you need a lawyer, Mr. Lawyer?" Emma's sarcastic words vibrated with anger. She stuck the Glock in his face. "Tell me who wanted my daughter. *Now!*"

"Em, calm down. I realize you want answers, but we have to do this the right way." Mason wanted this takedown to go by the book. They couldn't let anything fall through the cracks. "How did you find us?"

"Doesn't everyone know all the witness locations?"

Right, the safe house raids. Thankfully, they'd caught wind of the plan and moved every witness. "Tell us who leaked the information. If you do, we may see if we can get you a deal for your testimony."

The man sneered. "If I do, I'm as good as dead. You don't know the Luthers."

"So you admit they are behind this?" Emma asked.

Will flattened his lips.

The woman reappeared with the stroller.

Time to change locations. They were too out in the open. Mason grabbed Will's arm and lugged him from the bench. "Let's see if you'll talk at the station."

The woman's child wailed in the stroller. She stopped and leaned down to quiet her child. "Shh, sweetie. It's okay. How about a tune?" She pulled a tin whistle from her bag and played. She turned the musical instrument toward them and nodded before continuing on.

"Let's go." Mason pushed the man forward.

They walked for a few minutes until Will stumbled and dropped to the ground, struggling for breath.

Seconds later, his body convulsed before stilling.

"No!" Mason knelt beside him and listened to his breathing.

Silence.

He checked for a pulse.

Nothing.

Mason peered closer and noticed a tiny dart protruding from Will's neck.

He bolted upward. The woman must have poisoned him using her musical charade, fooling all of them. Had there even been a child in the stroller? All a ploy.

The Luthers had sent two assassins in case one failed.

Now Mason had no witness.

The pounding thrashing in Emma's ears confirmed her blood pressure had surged over the incident with Will Gowland and the unidentified female assassin who'd been hired to kill him. The ruthless Luthers would turn on family members, and that included any staff connected to them, if they suspected they'd been compromised. Mason had called his dad and given him the woman's description, but all they had to go on was a blond-haired female around five-six dressed in a jogging suit and baseball cap. Not enough information.

Emma rubbed her tummy, trying to relax the knot of frustration that had formed. They needed a break. She was tired of running. Tired of settling into a new place every day. Tired of the Luthers always being a mile ahead of them. When would it end?

How would it end?

She eyed her daughter sitting on the floor with a new puzzle spread out on the coffee table's wooden surface, singing her favorite song. At least she seemed content.

They'd moved to a two-bedroom cottage outside Niagara-on-the-Lake's town limits. One of her favorite places in Ontario. She wished she could take Sierra and explore the quaint and unique shops at the hamlet's center. One of her daughter's preferred stories, *Beauty and the Beast*, was playing at the local theatre. If only they were able to attend.

Mason entered the cottage after doing a perimeter sweep. "We're good. Nash parked along the street, and Lucas is around the corner." He sat and eyed Sierra. "Someone is happy even after having to leave the tire swing behind."

"Give her a puzzle and she's content." Emma rubbed her arm muscles. "I wish I could say the same thing. Mason, we need to end this."

"I know." He wrung his hands together. "I need to know who the leak is before we're compromised again."

"Any thoughts on who the mole is?"

"Deputy Rollins couldn't explain why his prints were on the tracker, so I can't rule him out. But I also don't like how Darlene's been acting and keeping information from me. Plus, she's suddenly gone MIA."

"Wait." Emma jumped up. "I just thought of the other evidence I forgot to share with you. Just a sec." She raced over to the box they'd been able to retrieve from the other safe house and pulled out a file. "Don't ask how I got the information."

Their fingers brushed as she handed him the paper. Her gaze snapped to his and held.

Did he feel their connection, too?

Even after fighting the attraction for days, she couldn't help the rush of feelings bombarding her. Their chemistry was undeniable.

Mason pulled away and stood, taking the paper.

A flush crept over her cheeks. Obviously, the emotions were one-sided. She squashed the disappointment. *Friends, Emma. That's all.*

Mason turned. "This is a list of all Luther Shipping's employee IP addresses. How did—"

"I told you not to ask and I realize it would be inadmissible in court, but I thought the information might help."

"Well, most IP addresses are dynamic and change."

"True, but it may still match the address used to put the earlier hit out," Emma pointed out. "What's the number again?"

Mason brought his computer to life and clicked the keys. "Okay, here it is. You check the sheet."

Emma grabbed the paper.

He read the number, and she ran her finger down the list. Would it match? "Say the address again."

He read it slower.

Her finger stopped. "Belongs to…" She gasped. "Who?"

"Lincoln Luther."

"How is that possible? He's in jail."

Emma sat. "Perhaps he ordered the hit from there. But why would his computer still be accessible?"

"They obviously thought he'd be back quickly, even though he'd been convicted."

Hope surged through her mind. Perhaps someone had slipped up within the organization. "Will this help tie him to the crimes?"

Mason closed his laptop. "We can't use the evidence, Em, as I suspect you got it through a hacker?"

She nodded and slumped in her chair. "Right." *Stupid, Emma.*

Mason's cell phone rang. "That's my father."

"Can you put him on speaker?"

He obliged. "Hey, Dad. I'm here with Emma."

"I have news, and it's not good."

Emma held her breath. *What now?*

"Lincoln Luther was just released from jail."

She bolted out of her chair.

Perhaps the crime lord had been behind everything. Even from prison.

TEN

Mason finished his father's call privately. The news had clearly shaken Emma, so he took his dad off speakerphone and continued the conversation. She had walked to the window in a daze and stared out into the yard.

That was ten minutes ago, and she still stood in the same place.

Mason approached and placed his hand at the small of her back. "Em, you okay?"

She jumped and pivoted, nostrils flaring. "What do you think? This will *never* be over." Her legs buckled, her CGM alarm sounding once again.

Mason grabbed her before she fell to the floor. "When was the last time you ate?" He lifted her into his arms and carried her to the couch.

"Mama?" Sierra dropped her puzzle pieces and ran to her mother.

"I'm okay, baby girl." She hugged her daughter, peering over her head. "Mason, can you get my medical bag from the kitchen table?"

She had been adamant about keeping her insulin within reach.

"On it." He carried it over and set it on the coffee table. Opening it, he brought out the necessary items.

After tending to Emma, he tucked Sierra in beside her mother and covered them both with an afghan. "You need to rest."

Emma's eyes drooped closed. "I'm sorry, Mason. I know this isn't your fault." She kept her voice level low.

"You don't need to apologize."

"What else did your dad say? How did Lincoln get released so early?"

How could he tell her it was possible some evidence her team had submitted may have been planted? Deciding never to hide anything from her, he pulled up a rocking chair and sat. "I'm sorry to have to tell you this, but apparently before Will died, he petitioned the courts and stated your team planted evidence."

She opened her eyes and propped herself against the pillows. "What? *Impossible.* We were thorough. What evidence?"

"The ledgers. How did you get them?"

"Someone within Luther Shipping sent them to the DA."

"Who?" he asked.

"Don't know. But when they received a warrant to search their financials, the ledgers proved to be accurate." Emma tucked the afghan closer to her sleeping daughter.

"They claim the police planted the evidence."

"No way would our task force have done that!"

"Em, please rest. We can talk about this later."

He got up and repositioned her pillows before gently kissing her forehead.

He snapped upright. Did he really just do that? It was an impulse and one that now felt comfortable. He checked for Emma's reaction but saw none.

She'd fallen asleep. Already.

Rain pelted the window. The weather turned the late-afternoon skies black, threatening another summer thunderstorm. *Not again.* He knew how much Sierra hated them, and this season they had been relentless. Hopefully she'd sleep through it. He closed the blinds to block out the sounds and pending lightning flashes. A question tumbled through his mind.

Was the storm a sign of more danger heading their way?

God's got this, Mason.

His mother's words popped into his head. Words she'd lived by, but ones he couldn't grasp. Not with all the tragedy happening in the world and in their own lives. His mother's death still hounded him even after ten years. *Why did You let her die, God?*

Mason studied Emma's beautiful face and Sierra sleeping soundly beside her mother. The little girl's mouth hung open, and cute snores filled the room. The desire to be their permanent protector overwhelmed him. But how could he do that without telling Emma his true feelings? She clearly only wanted to be friends.

He now wanted more than that, but could he

trust another woman after Zoe's betrayal? He'd vowed to never get involved again.

Emma is not Zoe.

The thought overwhelmed him, and he moved into the kitchen to work on his laptop. Time to focus his mind on solving the case or his feelings would consume him. He swiped at the screen and brought his computer to life. Clicking on his notes application, he reviewed his findings. Again.

Later that evening, after searching through Emma's files and exhausting all avenues, Mason sat with mother and daughter in front of the television watching *Beauty and the Beast*. Sierra giggled at something Chip said. A sound Mason now loved. It took his mind off the case. Unfortunately, he'd found nothing new. He had also called his father to get an update on the Luthers' current locations. His dad would contact the Buffalo PD to request they keep tabs on the trio. So far, Mason had received no word. It seemed all three had gone MIA…along with Darlene. He had to question why his partner had never told them about knowing Layla Luther.

Thankful for the much-needed break from his obsession over this case, Mason propped his feet on the ottoman and clasped his fingers together at the back of his head, leaning into the rocking chair. He could almost get used to this. Family gathered—

Lightning flashed, followed by an ear-piercing crack. The bolt made contact somewhere close.

Thunder shook the house, and seconds later the power snapped off, plummeting them into darkness.

Sierra screeched.

Not good. No power and a thunderstorm.

According to Emma, her daughter's worst fears—storms and darkness.

Mason stood slowly so he wouldn't further alarm the howling little girl. Emma tried to console her daughter, but it was no use. The combination of the storm and the power going out had taken her to a point of no return. He had to reassure them everything was okay. He fumbled his way into the kitchen and rummaged through the drawers until he found a flashlight.

His radio crackled, followed by garbled words. "Come again, Nash."

"Why are the lights off?" the deep voice repeated.

Emma shifted in her position and pulled Sierra closer. "Shh…baby girl. It's okay."

Mason's muscles hardened, and he rushed to the window. "He's right. The streetlights are on." He fingered the sidearm in his holster. "Emma, do you still have the Glock Dad gave you?"

She patted her pocket. "Yes."

"Good, stay here."

The flashlight's beam illuminated her widened eyes, glistening emeralds awakening his dormant heart.

Stop. Don't go there.

He turned away from her mesmerizing stare and grabbed the radio, speaking in a low voice. He moved out onto the porch. "Constable Nash, can you clear the area? Someone has taken out the power."

"I checked every nook of this cottage and the grounds just a few hours ago," the officer said.

"We can't risk it. I will stay with Emma and Sierra. I don't want them unguarded."

"Understood."

Mason walked back inside and shone his light into the living room. He eyed Jerome. Maybe it would help calm her again.

He grabbed the giraffe and wiggled it in front of the girl's face. "Jerome needs a hug." He played a game with the toy to entice her from her current state.

She stopped crying and hugged the stuffed animal.

Phew.

Mason moved back to the window and peered out, checking for any movement in the front yard. His cell phone rang. He pulled it from his pocket and checked the screen. "Dad, what's going on?"

"Son, Lance Luther was just spotted in the area. You need to be—"

The radio crackled. "Mason, the outage isn't from the storm. The power line was cut."

Had Lance found them?

* * *

Emma couldn't believe what she'd just heard. Someone had caused the power outage, and they were once again in trouble. She grabbed Sierra and bolted from the couch. They were running out of places to hide. The Luthers' resources seemed endless, and the crime family had proved they'd find them anywhere. What was even the point of running?

Sierra once again screamed in her arms, reminding Emma her daughter was the most important thing in the world to her. She had to protect her...at all costs. Even if that meant going on the run again.

"Where do we go, Mason?"

Another crack of thunder shook the cottage.

He raised his index finger as he spoke to his father. "Are you sure it's safe there, Dad? Shouldn't we get out of the province?"

No! She refused to be that far from her family, even though the WPP prevented her from seeing or talking to them while in the program.

"Okay, but that isn't very far from here," Mason said. "It's too close. Find another location."

Heated, muffled words filled the room, alerting Emma to her father-in-law's mood. He obviously didn't like his son challenging him.

Mason held the phone out and tilted his head. His father yelled. After Seth stopped, Mason put the phone back to his ear. "Fine, Dad. Do you trust this couple?"

What couple?

"Okay, we'll head there right away. I'll call you once we arrive." Mason hung up.

"Where are we going?"

"Dad's former partner owns a bed-and-breakfast a few towns over. He's offered us the place and his protection."

"Is it safe?" Emma set Sierra down and gathered the puzzle, her medical bag and Jerome.

"Chuck is aware of the situation. Dad trusts him with our lives. It's not a police-sanctioned safe house, and it's off the grid." Mason stuffed his laptop and papers into a duffel bag. "Chuck saved Dad's life when they worked together. They've kept in touch. His wife is a retired doctor."

"When can we stop running? We need to end this."

He walked over and moved a strand of hair out of Emma's eyes. "I know, Em. I want this to be over, too. You deserve to be happy and safe."

His woodsy scent tickled her sinuses. She could get lost in his nearness, but now wasn't the time. Maybe it never would be.

A knock jolted them from their conversation.

The interruption came at an appropriate time. She needed distance from her growing feelings for this man.

Mason stepped back and pulled out his Smith & Wesson.

"It's me," Constable Nash said. "Let me in."

Mason unlocked and opened the door. A blast of wind rushed at them, and he battled to shut the screen. "Did you find anyone?"

Nash stepped inside, water dripping from his hat. He took it off and wiped his face, then shook the rain from his windbreaker. "No, I didn't, but that doesn't mean they're not hiding close by. I'm here to escort you to your vehicle."

Mason holstered his weapon. "Dad called you?"

"Yes, and he's called Constable Lucas in, too. He'll be here any moment." He eyed Emma. "You need to get ready to move."

"Did Dad tell you where we're going?" Mason asked.

"No, which is odd. He told me he has your protection detail worked out and that Tom doesn't need to oversee securing the location."

Was her father-in-law referring to Chuck—the retired constable? How could he alone protect them from the Luthers when the entire police force hadn't been able to? Seth wasn't thinking straight, leaving them exposed with only an older man and woman. A shudder raced up Emma's spine and she swayed.

Mason grabbed her arm. "Em, it's okay. I won't let anything happen to you or Sierra."

A promise he shouldn't make. *Lord, haven't we been through enough already?*

"Em, get Sierra ready. Bring your medical bag, but only take—"

She waved her hands in the air. "I know. The necessities. Got it." She raced to the bedroom, regretting her harsh words to the man who only wanted to keep them safe. She needed to remain calm for Sierra's sake.

Five minutes later, Constable Nash opened the front door with his weapon raised.

A police cruiser pulled into the driveway.

"Tom is here. Let's check the grounds one more time." Nash disappeared into the darkness.

Another flash of lightning illuminated the area and exposed the rain pummeling sideways across the yard.

Sierra whimpered beside her.

Emma fastened her daughter's raincoat's hood tighter. "Baby girl, it's okay. I've got you." She took her hand.

The constables gave them the go-ahead to proceed.

Mason moved in front of them. "Stay behind me." He raised his gun and stepped into the rain. "Run."

Emma eyed the SUV at the end of the long driveway and squeezed Sierra's hand. "We need to run, baby girl, okay?"

Her daughter nodded.

They walked out from the sheltered porch, and the rain instantly soaked Emma's hair, matting it to her head. They raced down the steps but slipped on the last one.

Emma caught herself, but Sierra stumbled and fell. "Sierra!"

Mason turned and ran back toward them.

A split second later, the SUV exploded with a thunderous roar, taking out the police cruiser at the same time.

Flames ravaged both vehicles, and a chilling thought plowed through Emma's mind.

Sierra's fall had saved their lives.

ELEVEN

The blast shoved Mason forward, and he landed on his knees with a thud on the cottage's sidewalk. Thankfully, the cars weren't close to the house. Pain shot through him, and he winced not only from the injury but from the idea that the explosion had almost taken them out. He struggled to get up and fell again. He had to check on Emma and Sierra.

Protect them, Lord.

Mason inhaled deeply then pushed himself to his wobbly feet. Another flash of lightning revealed Emma lying on top of her daughter like an eagle protecting her baby under her massive wings. Constables yelled into their radios, requesting assistance.

Mason stumbled toward the girls. He must get them away from further harm. "Em. Sierra."

Emma sat up and rubbed her head. "Sierra, honey, wake up."

Her daughter lay motionless.

Dear God, no!

He fell to the ground beside them, ignoring the knifelike jabs shooting in his knees. "Sierra?" He felt for a pulse. Steady. He leaned down close to her mouth then inspected the back of her head. A slight bump had formed at the base of her skull. "She's breathing. I'm guessing she may have a bit of a concussion."

"Mason, save my baby girl!" Rain dripped from her quivering lips. "She's all I have."

You have me. He wanted to say the words out loud, but it wasn't the right time, and he doubted she would accept him after failing to protect them yet again.

Sirens pierced the night, but had the Luthers infiltrated all emergency services? Mason struggled to determine how the assailant had found them. Lucas had exited his cruiser before the explosion and stood next to Constable Nash at his unmarked SUV, talking into his radio.

Mason turned back to Emma. "Do you trust me?"

"Yes," she whispered.

"We're going to get Nash's keys and leave. Without any of them."

"Why aren't we waiting for the paramedics?"

He grabbed her arm. "I don't trust anyone at this point, and with Lance Luther in the area, it's not safe to stay here. We need to get to Chuck's. His wife can help with Sierra."

She nodded and stood.

Mason lifted Sierra and fumbled to his feet. He bit back the pain and stepped forward.

"What's wrong?"

"Hit my knee when the blast threw me. I'll be okay." He had to be…for their sake. "Let's go."

They approached Nash. "Help is on the way," the constable said. "Sierra okay?"

Flashing lights around the corner confirmed his statement.

Mason couldn't risk anything further. "Give Emma your keys."

"But—"

"Now. Remember who my father is."

Nash's eyes flashed with anger.

Mason hated to pull the dad card, but too much had happened in the past few days. They had to get away from everyone, including his father's men.

"Do it, Nash." Lucas pointed to his cruiser. "They can't use mine."

"Please," Mason bit out. "They're not safe here."

Nash handed the keys to Emma. "I hope you know what you're doing, Constable James."

So did Mason. "Thanks." He walked to the passenger side. "You drive," he told Emma. "I'll keep her in a tight hold."

She nodded and jumped in the driver's seat.

Mason climbed in, put his seat belt on and wrapped his arms around Sierra.

Multiple vehicles approached at high speed. "Head north."

She started the ignition and pulled onto the highway. "How far is this place?"

"Twenty minutes."

She accelerated.

"Don't go too fast on these wet roads. They're treacherous."

"I know how to drive, Mason. I've been trained, too." Her forced tone revealed her angst.

Right. He needed to trust in her abilities. He wouldn't do to her what his father had done to him—made him feel unworthy. "Sorry."

She rolled down her window a crack. "I need air before I hyperventilate."

The rain intensified as fork lightning flashed in the distance and made the dingy secondary highway even darker. The wipers oscillated, but not quickly enough to clear the windshield. Drops plopped through the open window.

They were in for a long twenty-minute drive.

Sierra stirred in his arms.

"Sisi, can you hear me?"

"Y'ncle Mason. My head hurts."

Emma reached over to her daughter. "Baby girl, you're going to be okay. Just hold on."

Sierra whimpered, and Mason held her tighter, praying his grip would reassure the four-year-old.

He glanced in the side-view mirror. Lights approached at full speed. Someone was following them. He pointed. "Emma, take that road."

She swerved and turned left.

The car followed.

"Someone's behind us. Go faster."

The tires hydroplaned, and the car lurched toward the ditch.

"Watch out!"

Emma turned the wheel to compensate, but it was too late. They were locked in a skid.

She hit the brakes, and the SUV struck muddy gravel before stopping just short of the embankment. She puffed out a ragged breath. "That was close."

A car door slammed.

Before Mason could reach for his gun, someone pounded on Emma's window.

Lance Luther stood beside them with an ominous stare.

Mason's muscles tensed at the sight of the crime boss's son, escalating his guard.

Emma's pulse ricocheted to her throat as her breathing came in rapid bursts. *Protect us from this madman, Lord.* She had to get them out of here. Emma gripped the steering wheel with her left hand and with her right put the car in Reverse. She stepped on the gas, but the tires spun in the mud. "I'll try rocking the car." She switched the gear into Drive and hit the accelerator. The car lurched slightly. She shifted to Reverse again and eased her foot onto the gas pedal.

Nothing.

They were stuck.

With a psychopath beside them.

Lance banged on the window. "I just want to talk."

"How can we believe that?" Emma glanced at Sierra. Her daughter's life was on the line, and she was at a loss on what to do. Sensing movement beside her, she glanced at Mason.

He pointed his weapon. "Emma, lean your head back so I can get a clear angle."

She obeyed.

"Let's not do this. A child's life is at stake, Luther." Mason's tone personified his intent.

To protect them both.

Lance raised his hands. "I'm unarmed. I would never hurt a child. I have two of my own. Open the door. Please."

His softened tone revealed his compassion for children. Could they trust him?

"Em, roll the window down farther."

She hit the button.

Rain splashed in her face. She ignored the stormy conditions and prayed for safety.

Lance wiped water from his face. "Please let me in. I'm soaked."

"Do it, Emma. I want to see what he has to say and ask about his company's bribes to those witnesses." Mason secured his free arm around Sierra. "He won't get to her. I promise."

She gripped the steering wheel tighter, frustration over the situation exploding through her body.

The desire to end his family's hold on her and Sierra trumped her decision. She unlocked the SUV.

Lance climbed into the back seat. "Thank you."

"Why are you here, Lance? To finish what your father started?" Mason's grated questions rushed out.

"To work together to bring him down."

Emma snapped her gaze to the sandy blond–haired man. "You expect us to believe you after everything your family has put us through?"

Lance removed his hood. "I don't blame you for not believing me, but my sister and I have called a truce."

"What do you want with us?" Mason shifted in his seat.

"Dad was released from prison, and we want to stop him from hurting any more people. It's time to put the family out of the crime business."

"Your sister told us the same thing over the phone today," Emma said.

"She mentioned you called. We're not behind this."

"If that's the case, then tell us who is and why your company tried to bribe witnesses at your father's trial," Mason said.

Lance's eyes widened.

Seemed they had caught him by surprise.

"That's a lie. My company did no such thing." His nervous voice raised a notch.

"We have the financial statements that prove otherwise," Emma said.

"Someone doctored our records. My business is legit. I am not my father."

Mason pointed the barrel of his gun over the top of the headrest. "What's stopping me from arresting you right now?"

"On what grounds? I've done nothing wrong." Sierra whined.

"Baby girl, it's okay. We're here." Would her words calm her daughter when Emma herself didn't believe it was okay?

Mason tucked Sierra tighter in his arms. "I've got you, Sisi." He turned back to Lance. "How can you help? Explain."

"By stopping whoever is behind this."

"And who exactly is that?"

"I can't tell you." He glanced out the window, evading their glare.

He was lying. Why?

"Can't or won't, Lance?" Emma asked.

He snapped his gaze back to her. "The less you know, the better. Plus, they'll kill me."

"We're only concerned about keeping our witnesses safe," Mason said.

"I get that. Don't you want this all to go away?"

Hope rose within Emma. "More than anything. I'm tired of running from your family, but I don't understand what you want us to do."

"Join me at a joint press conference in Buffalo.

Tell the world you're working with Layla and me to stop Dad's illegal business."

Mason whistled. "You're crazy. I'm not letting these two out of my sight."

"You don't have to. With you by their side, it would prove we're serious." He tapped his index finger on his chin. "Better yet, bring your chief superintendent father. That would solidify everything."

There was no way Seth James would agree to this man's terms. Not with his granddaughter's life in peril.

"How do you know so much about us?" Mason asked.

"I've done my homework." He glanced out the window again, but not before Emma caught a sneer slither across his face.

He was playing them. He was behind everything and just trying to get close to them. But why wouldn't he send his goons instead?

"If you and Layla are working together, why isn't she here, too?" Mason asked.

Good question.

"She's back home preparing for the press conference, getting everything into place."

Emma shifted in her seat. "Why are you *really* here?"

"And why target us and not the other witnesses?" Mason placed the barrel of his gun on the headrest.

"You two and your father have the biggest influence. Your cooperation would go a long way."

Emma was tired of this conversation. No way would she side with any Luther. Today or tomorrow. She didn't trust the entire family—even if they appeared to be legit.

Headlights approached around the curve on the otherwise quiet side road. The hairs at the back of her head prickled. Lance's presence was obviously a ruse to keep them in one place so someone could eliminate them.

And they'd fallen for his deception.

The truck slowed.

"Mason! It's a trick."

By the time she turned back around, Lance was pointing a gun at them. "I don't know who that is, I promise."

Mason raised his weapon. "We don't believe you."

Lance lunged forward and stuck the barrel against Emma's temple.

She froze.

"I'm telling you the truth, but I can see now this was a mistake. I'm not here to hurt you, but move one inch and I'll pull the trigger. My father taught me one good thing. How to shoot." With his left hand, Lance opened the door. "Don't follow me."

He jumped out and ran to his car.

The truck's window lowered, and a rifle's barrel peeked through.

"Gun!" Emma yelled. She ducked and thrust the gear into Drive, stepping on the gas and praying the tires would finally move.

The car lurched forward just as the back window shattered.

"Go! Go! Go!" Mason commanded. They needed to get out of this muddy rut if they were to survive. *Please, God. We need Your help.* Lance's motivation had to have been to keep them in one spot so his thugs could strike. It made sense. He wanted to get back into his father's good graces, and what better way to do that than take out the witnesses who put Lincoln Luther away? *You should've known better than to fall for it.* Some protector he turned out to be. Perhaps he should ask his father to put someone else on Emma's detail.

Yet there was just something about Lance's unexpected appearance tonight that raised a sliver of hope in Mason. Hope they'd solve this entire case, leaving Emma and Sierra safe and sound.

But would they still want him in their lives?

The tires spun but finally gained traction.

Emma maneuvered the SUV back onto the road and accelerated.

Mason glanced back to determine if the truck and Lance pursued them. The truck did a U-turn and followed, but Lance sped off in the opposite direction.

Odd.

Why not help the truck with the pursuit? Unless...

Unless he really *was* telling them the truth.

Mason doubted it, but the man's strange request piqued his interest. But for now, those thoughts would have to wait. "Faster, Emma. The truck is getting closer."

The rain had finally stopped.

Thankfully, Sierra had fallen back asleep. The little girl's resiliency amazed him.

Emma glanced over her shoulder, then back to the road ahead. "How can we lose them?"

They sped by a marker sign for an upcoming town. One and a half kilometers. An idea formed. "Take the next exit, but wait until the last second. We can hide in the village."

She nodded and kept her gaze focused on the curvy road.

Moments later, he spotted the sign. "There's the exit. I'll tell you when to turn."

She twisted her grip on the steering wheel.

"You can do this." He sneaked a peek in the side-view mirror. The truck approached faster. Good. Their surprise exit would help. He waited for the opportune time. "Now."

Emma swerved the SUV onto the ramp at the last minute.

The truck sped by, missing their turn.

"Yes!" Mason pounded the dashboard. "Go right. That will take us into the town."

She obeyed.

He guided her through the small downtown until they came to an alleyway. "Turn left." Mason searched for the perfect spot and noticed a parking garage. He pointed. "There. We can hide here."

She pulled into the structure.

"Drive up a couple of floors and park behind a barrier."

A minute later, they sat in a hidden spot.

"How long do we wait?" Emma asked.

He leaned over and glanced at the digital clock on the dashboard. Nine thirty p.m. "I'm going to get Dad to send police to the area. That should deter them if they circle back to search for us." He put his weapon away and fished out his phone, punching in his father's number.

"Son, where are you? Nash told me about the explosion earlier. Chuck called and said you hadn't arrived yet."

"We had an issue after we left the cottage."

"An issue?" Seth asked.

"Yes. A visit by Lance Luther."

His father huffed in a breath. "What happened?"

He explained the impromptu meeting with the crime family's son.

"There's no way I would have sanctioned the press conference."

"I know, Dad. We feel his visit was a ruse to

keep us in one place to allow his men to take us out." He told him about the truck and their pursuit but how they'd lost them and were now hiding. "Can you have constables come to the town and tell them to keep an eye out for a silver pickup truck? It was too dark and rainy to catch the plate number. That should deter them from looking for us."

"On it."

"We'll wait here until you give us the go-ahead to proceed to Chuck's."

"Stay safe." His father clicked off.

Emma leaned her head back and inhaled deeply.

"You okay?"

"My breathing is off. I need to steady it." She turned her head to face him. "That was too close." She breathed in and exhaled slowly through her mouth multiple times.

"Anything I can do for you?"

"I'll be fine." She caressed Sierra's face. "This one surprises me all the time. She hates storms, but here she is sleeping soundly."

"I guess we tuckered her out." He glanced at his watch. "Hopefully, Dad gives us the all clear to head to Chuck's soon. I just don't want to come out of hiding if that truck is near."

"Do you believe what Lance said?"

"No, but I noticed instead of pursuing us, he headed in the opposite direction. Not sure why."

"Nothing surprises me with the Luthers. I caught

him sneering at one point. He's up to something. My guess is Layla didn't even know he was here."

Mason flexed his fists. "I need this to end or Dad will never forgive me for not solving the case."

Emma touched his arm. "Will you tell me what's going on between you and your father? Why don't you get along? I know you didn't share the entire story with me earlier."

He sighed. Should he bare all now? It wasn't like they had anywhere to go at the moment. "Brady didn't tell you?"

"Tell me what?"

The image of his mother's lifeless eyes flashed before him. The day forever etched in his mind. "I blame Dad for Mom's death."

"But I thought she died from a burglary gone wrong. How was that Seth's fault?"

"That's the fable my father spun to the media. He wouldn't admit he put his own wife in harm's way." The lingering anger creeping through his voice surprised him even after ten years. He clearly hadn't dealt with it as much as he thought.

"What?"

"Dad was close to bringing down a drug king-pin along with the task force he was on. Mom had complained about hang-ups on their landline, but Dad brushed it off to wrong numbers. It was like he was too proud to admit someone had targeted our family." Tears welled, and he rubbed his eyes to force them back. He still missed his mother. Every day.

"What happened?"

"I pleaded with him to plant someone in the house to watch over Mom, but he wouldn't hear of it. Said no drug leader would dare step foot in the Jameses' home. Instead, he agreed to have an officer drive by on a rotating schedule."

"What did your mother say about the situation?" she whispered.

"She hadn't heard the extent of his involvement. He was always strict about how much information he shared on his cases."

"How did the intruder get in?"

"Posed as a deliveryman, and Mom opened the door." He released a sharp breath. "She didn't even make it to the kitchen. Shot her in the entryway."

"I'm so sorry."

A tear escaped. "If only I'd gotten there five minutes before."

She straightened in her seat. "You found her? Brady never told me."

"Yes. She had asked me to come for lunch, and I was five minutes late. I blame myself, too. Every day." Another tear rolled down his cheek. The earlier adrenaline rush crashed and caused his emotions to crumble.

Emma leaned closer and wiped away the tears, her fingers lingering. "Mason, it's not your fault.

You could never have predicted something like this would happen."

He covered her hand with his and eyed her lips, wondering what it would be like to kiss her.

A small gasp escaped her mouth, but she stayed close.

Did she feel it, too? Was it possible she wanted to be more than friends? Dare he even go there? She was his brother's wife. Then there was Zoe's betrayal…

But he could no longer deny his feelings. He had to tell her about Zoe. "Did Brady ever tell you about my relationship with a woman named Zoe?"

"Not everything." She averted her gaze.

Not before he spotted something in her expression, but he struggled to identify the emotion. "When I lived in Nova Scotia, I met Zoe Dickerson. I fell fast for her, and we became close. I trusted her when she asked me for help."

"What do you mean?"

"She said she was behind in her mortgage payments and would lose her house. Plus her credit cards were maxed out. I gave her twenty-five thousand dollars to help." He dug his fingernails into his palms, reliving the moment. "The next day when I went to visit her, she was gone. The neighbor told me Zoe had left in the middle of the night and she didn't own the house. She played me bigtime. What kind of cop lets someone do that to them?"

Again, she caressed his cheek. "A kindhearted one. It could happen to the best of us."

He searched her emerald eyes for a sign of disgust but found none. He inched closer. "Em, I—"

His cell phone buzzed.

Emma jumped back and gazed out the window.

He glanced at the screen. It was his father giving them the all clear to head to Chuck's.

Maybe it was for the best.

Keep your head in the game.

It wasn't his head he worried about.

His heart was long gone.

TWELVE

Emma turned into the entrance of Chuck's Hideout thirty minutes later. She suppressed a chuckle at the irony surrounding the B&B's name. The SUV's tires crunched on the gravel as she drove down the long tree-lined driveway. The Victorian home sat nestled deep into the woods, true to its name. A great place to hide. Emma prayed that was true.

She and Mason had remained quiet on the drive after their explosive moment earlier. She resisted the urge to touch her lips at the thought of his on hers. Had he been about to kiss her? How did she feel about that?

Face it, you wanted him to. A question lingered—would his lips feel different from his brother's? Brady's kisses changed a year into their marriage. The tender ones turned rough and abusive. Mason's had to be different. Warmth flushed her cheeks, and for once she was thankful for the darkness concealing her emotions.

Sierra stirred and sat up in Mason's arms, intruding on Emma's thoughts. Thankfully.

She parked in front of the well-lit home. "Baby

girl, this is where we'll be staying next." She glanced at her daughter.

Sierra's mouth formed an O before she buried her face in Mason's chest. "It's scary, Mama."

Emma studied the two-story home, complete with a turret. Clear lights had been strung along both levels and around each window, creating an eerie ambience. Her daughter told the truth—the house did give off that vibe. Emma loved Victorian homes and couldn't wait to see the inside. How many families had lived in this unique house and what were their stories? She surmised the building held many secrets from past generations—something that fascinated Emma. She loved to delve into historical events. Maybe they'd even find a hidden room or two.

"It's okay, Sierra. It's just a really old home." She turned off the ignition. "Time for bed."

A man dressed in overalls and ball cap, with a hankie protruding from his front pocket, stepped onto the porch, rifle in hand.

Sierra whimpered.

Emma glanced at Mason. "Help, please."

Mason nodded and unbuckled his seat belt. "Let me go first. Sisi, you stay here." He stepped outside and moved Sierra onto the seat.

Mason approached the man. Seconds later, the older gentleman tucked the rifle back inside the door. Mason turned and waved them in.

"Let's go, baby girl. Uncle Mason says everything is okay."

Her daughter hesitated.

Emma stepped from the SUV, walked around to the passenger side and lifted Sierra into her arms. "I've got you."

The duo walked up the steps and onto the veranda.

"Emma, this is Chuck Evans." Mason turned to the gray-haired man. "Chuck, Emma and Sierra James."

She waved. "Thank you for letting us stay here. We appreciate it."

"You're very welcome. Anything for good ole Sethy. He had my back on many occasions. It's the least I could do." Chuck squeezed Sierra's nose and held up his fisted hand with his thumb protruding. "Got your nose."

She giggled.

"Did Seth send his team to get your house prepared?" Emma asked.

"No need. We're fully stocked. Plus, we have surveillance equipment and cameras on the property." He hooked his thumbs in his overall bib. "Call it a retired cop's paranoia. Can't be too careful these days."

"That's a good thing in this case," Mason said.

The wooden screen door opened, and a petite woman stepped outside. The door slammed shut behind her.

Sierra jumped in Emma's arms.

"Sorry, been meaning to fix that spring," Chuck said. "This is my wife, Irene." He introduced them all.

"Let's get you inside." The sixtysomething honey brown–haired woman guided Emma and Sierra to the door. "You must be exhausted. Chuck explained what's been happening."

Just how much had Seth shared? Wasn't her case classified?

"Yes, it's been a rough few days," Emma admitted. "Plus, we're all still damp and grungy from the thunderstorm."

"I have a special antique tub," Irene said. "All my guests love it, along with the soothing bath bombs I make. You and Sierra will be on the second level. I have the perfect room set aside. It has an adjoining door into the next room, but no one is staying there."

"Why don't you have any guests?"

She led them through the kitchen and dining room to the mahogany staircase. "Seth didn't tell you?"

"No. What?"

"He paid for us to move all our guests to a fancy hotel back in town. On his own dime. He wanted you to have the place to yourselves with Chuck here to help protect you."

Sierra rubbed the back of her head. "Mama, my head hurts."

Right. The blast. How could Emma have forgotten? *What kind of mother am I?* "Irene, Seth said you're a retired doctor. Sierra took a fall after the car exploded. Can you check her over?"

"Certainly. Let's go to your room." She climbed the stairs.

Emma followed, admiring the artwork along the way.

Forty-five minutes later, she climbed into bed alongside her daughter. Her weary muscles screamed at her, and she longed for rest. Would she be able to wind down after such a tough day?

Irene had thoroughly checked Sierra and stated the four-year-old had no signs of a serious head injury.

Thankfully.

Lance's peculiar visit rolled over and over in her mind, which refused to shut down.

Creak. Creak.

Emma bolted upward in bed.

A shadow passed under the door and stopped at her room. Her breath hitched.

A gentle knock followed. "Em?"

Emma blew out the breath she'd been holding and jumped out of bed. She opened the door.

Mason stood in plaid pajama bottoms, a navy blue T-shirt hugging his muscles, and bare feet.

Once again, her breath hitched, but not out of fear this time. Could he be any more gorgeous?

"You scared me," she whispered.

"Sorry. Just wanted to make sure you and Sierra were settled in. I know this old house is odd."

She smiled. "I love it. We're fine. You heading to bed?"

"Yes. I'm downstairs if you need anything." He moved his big toe in a circle. "About earlier—"

"Don't, Mason. I can't."

An emotion settled in his hazel eyes.

Disappointment?

He glanced downward. "Understood. Night." He walked away.

Had she just crushed his possible feelings for her?

It was for the best.

At least, that's what she told herself, but her heart disagreed.

Mason was grateful the next two days passed without incident. They needed rest from the mayhem. Even though the older home had spooked Sierra when they first arrived, she now loved running through the halls and up to the turret. She even ventured into the attic with her mother. This morning on his perimeter sweep, he spotted the little girl perched at the top window while Emma read to her.

A sight he loved, but Emma's words about their almost kiss had trampled any hope he had of a future with them. He knew it was for the best, but why did it hurt so much? Had he really fallen that hard, so quickly?

He wanted a wife and family. *This family.* A question nagged him.

Would Brady approve?

Well, it didn't matter, because Emma had made herself clear the other night. They'd only be friends. He should've known better than to open his heart a crack after the damage Zoe had inflicted. Hadn't he learned his lesson the first time?

Well, no more. He put his walls up for good this time.

Mason cleared the surroundings of any suspicious activities and walked into the antique-adorned dining room. The aroma of roasted coffee wafted from the kitchen, and he hurried to grab a cup. He needed caffeine to kick-start his adrenaline and stop his foul mood. His cell phone rang, and he pulled it from his back pocket. He set it on the counter and hit the speaker button. "Hey, Dad. What's up?"

"There's been a development. We found the truck from the other night when someone took a shot at you."

Mason poured the liquid and added creamer. "Where?"

"They abandoned and torched the truck outside the town you hid in. Here's the interesting part. Local police found it before everything was destroyed. We have a plate number."

Mason took a sip and carried his phone to the dining room table. "Who's it registered to?"

"Matt Abbott."

"Abbott? Why does the name sound familiar?"

"He's been in and out of jail for multiple reasons," his father told him. "Drugs, car theft, assault. His sister is Nadine Abbott."

"Who's that?"

"Right. You were undercover and wouldn't know. Nadine is Darlene's newest CI."

Mason plunked himself into the chair. *"What?"*

"I told you it was interesting. Sending you Nadine and Matt's pictures to see if you recognize them."

His phone dinged, and he switched the screen to view the photos. He zoomed in on the woman.

And almost dropped his coffee mug.

"Dad, that's the woman who took out Will Gowland with the poisoned dart."

The pitter-patter of footsteps told Mason that Sierra and Emma were coming down the stairs. He picked up his phone, taking his father off speaker.

"I'll put a BOLO out on her and Matt," his dad said. "Maybe we'll catch a break."

"Don't you think it's odd this woman is a hired assassin by the Luthers *and* connected to Darlene? Do you still trust her?"

"Honestly, I don't know what to believe anymore," Seth admitted.

His dad was right. Too much had happened in the past few days to figure it all out.

"Where is she?" Mason asked.

"I'm concerned the Luthers got to her. I have my men searching."

Sierra ran into the room. "Y'ncle Mason." She flew to him and latched onto his legs.

He chuckled and tousled her red locks. "Hey, Sisi."

"Is that my Tiddlywinks? Can I talk to her?"

"Sure." He held the phone to Sierra's ear. "Your grandfather wants to talk to you."

Her eyes lit up, and she grabbed the phone. "Poppie! You coming for breakfast?"

Mason glanced at Emma. "Her speech has improved."

"It's your influence."

He quirked a brow, tilting his head. "Why would you say that?"

"I think you remind her of Brady. Even though she was young when he died, she remembers his voice. *Your* voice."

Their parents had always confused them when they were growing up. Brady was only a year younger than Mason. People often called them by the wrong name. Maybe it was a saving grace with Sierra, to help improve her vocabulary so she could play well with other kids. If they could ever settle in one place long enough to make friends.

Sierra chatted nonstop with his dad while Mason filled Emma in on Darlene's CI being the assassin.

"Can we tie her to the Luthers?" Emma asked, walking into the kitchen.

He followed.

She poured herself a cup of coffee.

"I'll get Dad working on it." He topped off his mug. "Irene makes the best coffee."

"Agreed. She roasts her own beans." Emma walked back into the dining room. "Sierra, time to let Poppie get back to work."

Later that day after supper, Mason settled in the den and clicked the television channel to a hockey game, hoping to unwind. The girls had gone to bed early. Mason and Chuck had done a final sweep of the property, but Mason wanted to stay up to provide protection. His gut told him the assassin was close. Why he believed that, he didn't know.

Right now everything was as quiet as a cat stalking a mouse. He leaned his head back and closed his eyes, listening to the announcer's play-by-play.

An alarm sounded, piercing the night.

Mason bolted upright. He'd fallen asleep and let his guard down.

Why can't you do anything right?

His father's words from Mason's childhood had

followed him into adulthood and still tormented him. He'd failed at protecting his mother and now Emma.

Chuck bounded into the room, rifle in hand. "We need to check the security monitors. Let's go."

Mason followed him from the den into Chuck's man cave, which was equipped with every gadget, including monitors surveilling the property.

"Someone tripped the system." The man slammed his palm on the table. "They thought they could get by ole Chuckie. Fooled them." He hit a switch, and the whirling alarm stopped.

Mason peered closer at each screen, checking for perpetrators. "Do you see anyone? Could an animal have triggered the alarm?"

"I set the traps so animals wouldn't be detected unless it's a bear." He sat and clicked the keyboard. "Let's see what we have."

The screens switched to a different area as Chuck moved to each camera.

"What's going on?" Emma leaned on the door frame, Glock at her side.

"Someone tripped the alarm," Mason said. "We're just trying to see where they are on the property."

"There!" Chuck yelled. "East entrance."

All three of them peered closer.

A ponytail bounced as the woman turned.

Nadine Abbott.

She'd come to finish the job.

THIRTEEN

Emma stumbled backward and grabbed the wall to steady herself. How had this woman known their location? Seth had assured them this hideout was off the beaten path. Emma sank into a chair. Maybe she should flee the country, but she now realized they wouldn't be safe anywhere. Not with Lincoln Luther a free man and multiple assassins at his beck and call. "Mason, how do the Luthers keep tracking us?"

He scratched his head. "I have no idea. It makes little sense. No one knows Dad's and Chuck's affiliation other than—"

"Other than your father's force." Chuck finished Mason's sentence. "Didn't you say a constable is missing?"

"Yes, my partner, Darlene." He crossed his arms.

Emma didn't miss the contorted expression on his handsome face. He still didn't trust his partner, and the fact she was MIA had obviously riled him.

Emma turned her gaze to the monitor and jumped up.

The woman no longer appeared on the screen.

"Where did she go?" Stars danced in her eyes as her legs wobbled. "I need to get back to Sierra."

Chuck stood, picked up his rifle and grabbed the radios. "Let's go hunting, Constable."

Mason pulled out his Smith & Wesson. "We can't leave Emma, Irene and Sierra."

A slam of a shotgun racking sounded behind him.

They turned.

Irene held her weapon across her body, the gun nearly overpowering the petite woman. "They won't get by me."

"That's my girl," Chuck said.

Irene pointed at Emma's Glock. "I assume you know how to use that."

"Of course," she said.

"You boys go. Catch the creep." Irene moved to the front door and peered out.

Had Emma just walked onto the set of a bad Western? If the situation wasn't so precarious, she would laugh, but right now her rigid muscles had her guard elevated.

Mason grabbed her arm. "Will you be okay?"

She nodded and prayed her demeanor didn't betray how she really felt at the moment. Emma willed her wobbly legs to move forward. *You can do this.* She wouldn't let anyone get to her daughter.

They moved into the foyer.

"Irene, bolt the door behind us and don't open it until you see it's us." Chuck handed her a radio. "Keep in constant contact."

The men left.

"I need to check on Sierra." Emma bolted up the stairs, two at a time, and dashed to the room. She eased the door open with her gun raised. She needed to be prepared for anything.

Her daughter slept soundly. How did the alarm not wake her?

Emma checked all the windows before backing out of the room and closing the door.

She hurried down the stairs just as a shot rang out. She stumbled on the last step but caught herself.

Mason!

Her chest constricted, her mouth suddenly dry. Had he been shot?

She darted back to the security monitors and discovered Irene flipping to each screen until she found the men.

Chuck knelt beside the woman's body with his fingers on her neck and shook his head.

Mason spoke on the phone.

Emma blew out a massive breath. *Thank God you're okay, Mason.*

What would she have done if he had been killed?

The thought of losing him froze her. Were her feelings for him stronger than she'd thought?

"They got her." Irene fist-pumped her hand in the air. "I knew she wouldn't get by my man."

If only they could keep the woman alive to question her and see who had ordered their deaths.

An answer Emma longed for to put this all behind them and go back to her normal life.

If that would ever be possible.

Glass shattered upstairs.

Followed by her daughter's scream.

Pain clutched her chest. "Sierra!" She raced up the stairs, Irene at her heels.

"Chuck, someone's in the house," the older woman said into the radio. "Get back here. Now!"

Had they somehow missed another intruder? Was Nadine a distraction while the other assassin sneaked into the house via the rickety balcony stairs?

Rustling and faint screams sounded behind the bedroom door. Someone muzzled her daughter.

"I'll sneak through the adjoining door. Catch them by surprise," Irene whispered. She grabbed Emma's hand. "Don't worry, Chuckie trained me well. My paranoid hubby wanted me to be able to defend myself in any situation."

Good thing.

Emma waited for Irene to enter the other bedroom before easing Sierra's door open.

A bushy-bearded man wearing a bandanna over his head stood beside the bed and held Sierra in a firm grip.

Emma stepped inside, gun raised. "Let. My. Daughter. Go." Her words announced her intent. She would not let anything happen to Sierra, even if it meant Emma had to pay the price with her own life. Sisi was not leaving with this man.

The man moved closer to the window he'd entered through and pointed the gun in Sierra's temple. "Put your gun down or she dies."

Pounding footsteps entered the lower level.

Mason and Chuck had heard Irene's cry for help, but would they make it in time to save Emma's daughter? She had to stall.

"Who hired you?" she asked.

"Do you think they want you to know that? I'm not stupid. I know what they do to people who betray them."

"The Luthers? Which one?"

"I ain't saying nothin'."

Sierra squirmed in his arms, screaming behind the man's hand.

"Baby girl, it's gonna be okay." Emma took another step and in her peripheral vision caught the adjoining door easing open. "Why take my daughter? Why not just kill me? I'm the threat to them, not her."

Creak.

The men were on the stairs. Closer. *Thank You, Lord.*

"I never said it was the Luthers. The dark web instructions said to get the girl. They want her alive."

Emma swallowed her surprise.

Why would they want Sierra unharmed? To take revenge on Emma? Or something else?

"Give it up, Matt!" Mason's voice boomed behind her. "There's nowhere to run. Nadine is dead."

The man's eyes flashed venom in the dimmed lighting. "Did you kill her, Constable James?"

The side door burst open, and Chuck aimed his rifle at Matt. "No, I did."

The man turned. It was enough of a distraction. Sierra bit Matt's hand.

He yelled and loosened his grip, allowing the little girl to kick him. He released her, and she fell to the floor. "Why, you brat!" He lifted his gun toward Sierra.

Emma fired her weapon at the same time as Mason.

Matt Abbott crumpled to the floor.

Mason raced to the sobbing Sierra and gathered her into his arms. "It's okay, Sisi. I've got you." *Thank You, Lord, for protecting us today.* Even though Mason had been angry with God for years, his childhood faith came back to him now. Could he finally trust in the One he assumed had betrayed him?

Matt stirred. How had the multiple shots not killed the man?

Mason passed Sierra over to Emma. "Take her downstairs."

She nodded and rushed out of the room with Irene close behind.

Chuck knelt beside Matt. "How did you find us?"

The man sneered.

Chuck pressed on his wound.

Matt screamed.

"Not so funny now, huh?" Chuck asked. "Tell us and we'll get the paramedics here to save your life." He pressed again.

Matt's eyes bulged. "Coordinates on the dark web."

Mason leaned closer. "Who ordered you to take the girl?"

"Not. Sure. Signed Luther Shipping." Matt coughed.

Mason glanced at Chuck. "The Luthers. Same MO as last time."

Lance must have found their location and put it on the web. Mason had a hard time comprehending how this family always managed to stay a step ahead of them.

"He's not going to tell us any more." Mason stood and pulled out his cell phone. "I'm calling Dad to get—"

Matt coughed again, his breathing sounding the rattle of death. He was out of time.

A moment later, his body stilled, his lifeless eyes staring at the ceiling.

Chuck's shoulders slumped. "Looks like we need the coroner instead."

Mason punched in his father's number and waited.

"Son, what's going on?" His dad's groggy voice told Mason he'd been asleep.

Mason checked his watch. Two fifteen a.m. He put it on speakerphone. "Sorry to wake you. I have you on speaker here with Chuck. We had an incident." He explained about the two assassins. "How do they keep finding us?"

"No idea. I'll get the coroner there, stat. How did they get by you?"

In other words, his son couldn't protect his granddaughter.

Not that he didn't agree, but did his father have to be so blatant about it? *Why am I surprised?* His dad had been like that throughout Mason's life, so there was no reason it would be any different now.

Mason gripped the cell phone tighter and counted to ten under his breath. "Dad, these people are ruthless. They know what they're doing."

"Seth, he's right. They had obviously staked the place out. They tripped my one alarm, which alerted us. Your son helped take out both creeps. You taught him well."

At least someone appreciated his abilities.

"Dad, let us know what you find out," Mason said.

"I'll get back to you. Resecure the premises and I'll have a constable there right away." He hung up.

Chuck stood and squeezed Mason's shoulder. "Son, your dad does believe in you."

"He has a funny way of showing it."

"If it's any consolation, he has all the newspaper clippings from your arrests on the East Coast in his office desk drawer. I saw them."

He does?

"Well, I wished he'd stopped pressing so hard." Mason walked to the broken window and peeked out. The moon glowed, illuminating the backyard as an owl hooted from a nearby tree. He understood why Chuck had moved here. The serenity would allure anyone.

Sierra and Emma loved the country lifestyle. If only—

Stop, Mason.

"I don't understand how our location keeps getting compromised," he said. "We've been so careful, but we can't plug the leak. Someone on the force must be helping the Luthers." He explained about Jerome's tracking device.

"Could they have put a tracker on anything else? Did Emma take any other personal belongings?"

A flash of her fingering her heart locket hovered in his mind. "Wait. Dad let her keep a necklace her mother gave her." He ran out of the room and down the stairs.

He found Emma sitting in the living room, rocking Sierra as she sang to her.

The scene took his breath away, and he hated to interrupt. He stepped into the room. "Em, can you give me your necklace?"

She stopped singing. "Why?"

"I'm concerned it's how they're tracking us."

Her eyes widened. "Like Jerome."

"Yes."

She lifted her hair up. "Can you take it off? Sierra just fell asleep and I don't want to wake her."

Mason walked behind and gently unfastened the necklace. Her body trembled beneath his fingers.

Was it from his touch, or had she caught a chill?

"You got it?" she asked.

He set aside his unanswered question and stepped back in front of her, examining the locket. "Yes. It's stuck."

"I haven't been able to open it for some time now."

He tugged harder, but the hinge wouldn't budge. Mason held it closer to the light. A small bead of dried glue lined the edge. "Someone sealed it shut."

"What?"

Mason glanced around the room and eyed a sewing basket beside the rocking chair. He opened it and pulled out small scissors. "I'll try my hardest not to scratch it, as I know this is from your mom."

"Thank you."

He gently sliced through the glue, and the locket popped open. A small tracking device fell to the floor.

His hunch was correct. Someone had also bugged the locket.

Which meant they would need to run.

Again.

Emma jumped out of the rocking chair, disturbing Sierra. She scolded herself for reacting too quickly and placed her daughter on the couch. "Sorry, baby girl. Go back to sleep." She tucked a blanket on top of her, then turned to Mason. "How did they get at the locket?"

He snapped the device in two. "Do you remember if you ever took the chain off? Maybe to bathe or shower?"

She shook her head. "I vowed to myself I would never do that. Mom gave it to me as a high school graduation gift." She racked her brain. How had they gotten to her prized possession? *Think, Emma. Think.*

She snapped her fingers. "The clasp broke a few weeks back, and I left it on the kitchen counter until your father could bring me some tools to fix it." She plunked herself back into the rocker. "Mason, someone on your dad's team is leaking information."

"Was Darlene with you at that point?"

"Yes. She'd just been tasked to me."

Mason clenched his fists. "We have to find her."

"Where could she be?" Emma buried her face in her palms. "I can't take this any longer."

Mason knelt in front of her and took her hands in his. "Em, I will be with you until this is over. You have my word."

She gazed into his softened eyes. "Thank you. I don't know what Sierra and I would do without you."

"I'm so sorry I stayed away from you both after Brady died."

She pulled one hand away and caressed his face. "You're here now. That's what matters most. He was proud of you."

"I still miss him."

Emma loved this man's kind heart. So different from his brother's. Dare she tell him the truth? "I need to tell—"

Chuck cleared his throat. "Sorry to interrupt."

Mason lurched to his feet. "What's going on?"

"I found their vehicle on the edge of the property. They cut the south-side fence."

"I'll get Dad to run the plates," Mason said. He held up the broken tracker. "This is how they found us." He stuffed it back in his pocket.

"Still don't know how they breached the property," Chuck muttered. "The scoundrels."

A car door slammed.

Chuck moved to the window. "Coroner and a police cruiser are here."

Mason's cell phone buzzed. He pulled it out. "Dad calling."

"I'll let them in." Chuck left the room.

Mason answered the call. "What's going on, Dad?" A pause. "Yes, she's here." He hit the speaker button.

Emma got up and stood beside Mason. "Hey, Seth."

"I have news. Lincoln Luther was just found dead outside his penthouse building."

"What?" Mason said. "How?"

"Appears he jumped. Left a suicide note."

Emma blanched, her hand flying to her chest. *Impossible.*

FOURTEEN

Mason caught the grimace on Emma's confused face. "What is it, Em?"

"There's no way he killed himself," she said.

Mason guided her to the chair. "Why do you say that?"

"Because I studied the man inside and out. He was too arrogant to take his own life."

"Dad, have authorities check to be sure," Mason said.

"I've already asked Buffalo PD to take a second look. They said they'd get back to me. This may finally be the end of this madness."

Mason crammed his hand into his pocket and fingered the tracker. "Dad, any headway in discovering Darlene's whereabouts?" He explained the device they'd found in Emma's locket.

"Nothing. Her sister said she brought her son over and then left early a few mornings ago. She hasn't returned. Odd. We've officially launched a missing-person report."

Had the woman been abducted? Or had Darlene suspected they were on to her, so she fled?

Questions Mason needed answered.

"Keep us posted." Mason glanced at Emma. She rubbed her eyes.

There was no way he'd ask her to run if this was finally over. "We're going to remain at Chuck's until we confirm."

"Understood." He hung up.

"Thanks, Mason, for letting us stay here. I'm tired of running." Emma leaned back in the chair. "I want to fight back."

Chuck passed the living room with the coroner and walked up the stairs. Constable Nash stood in the living room entryway, gesturing Mason to come.

"I understand. You're frustrated and want this over." Mason grabbed another blanket and placed it around her. "Why don't you rest? I need to talk to Nash."

She nodded and shut her eyes.

Mason tiptoed from the room and followed the other man outside.

Crickets chirped as fireflies lit up the property. How he'd love to be out camping somewhere. It was a perfect night. Cool enough for sleeping, but still warm inside a tent.

"Mason, your dad filled me in," Nash said. "I want you to know I have your back. I am not the leak."

At this point, Mason still couldn't trust anyone. Not even his father's men, but he wouldn't admit it to Nash. "I appreciate that. What do you have for me?"

He gestured toward the south corner. "I want to show you something in the vehicle."

Mason followed the constable to the property's edge and ducked to step through the cut fence. A blue four-wheel-drive truck was parked beside an enormous oak tree.

Nash opened the passenger-side door and pulled out a file, handing it over. "I found this when I looked through the truck."

Mason opened the folder. A dossier file, including Emma's and Sierra's information and pictures. Along with coordinates of Chuck's B&B. "There's nothing here saying who ordered the hit, but we suspect it's the Luthers."

Nash opened the rear door. "Look at this."

Mason stepped closer.

The back seat held enough ammunition for a small war.

He whistled. "Where would they have gotten all this?"

"I'm guessing on the black market." Nash fished cards from his pocket. "I also found these in the glove box." He held his hand out.

Business cards for Constables Darlene Seymour and Tom Lucas.

"What?" Heat fueled inside his body, turning his blood to a boiling point. *Rein in your emotions, Mason.* "How could they betray us? Is Dad aware?"

"Yes, I called him first. He's questioning Tom

himself." Nash checked his watch. "He's probably doing that right now. However, Darlene is still in the wind."

Were they both in on it together? Seemed unreasonable, but the Luthers' money easily tantalized and took no prisoners.

"You know Tom better than I do. Do you really believe he's the leak?" Mason asked.

The other man glanced away. "I hope not, but he confided in me his wife took him to the cleaners in the divorce settlement."

"And Darlene?"

"Just started working with her on a regular rotation." Nash leaned against the truck. "You were partners. What's your guess?"

"I've only known her for two years, and one of those I spent undercover." A thought lingered. *How well do you really know someone?*

Mason flipped the dossier to the last page and inhaled sharply. It also held a photo of Skip Perry. His CI. "They were the ones who took out my informant." He held the picture up.

Breath hissed through Nash's teeth. "Well, I'll be a monkey's uncle."

"Nadine also took out Will Gowland. Did we ever find out the poison used in the dart?"

"Yes, high levels of cyanide."

"No wonder it worked so quickly. He didn't stand a chance of survival." Mason's cell buzzed. He glanced at the number.

Unknown.

"I need to take this. Be right back." He walked down the road and hit Answer. "Mason here."

"Constable James, it's Deputy Darryl Rollins."

Mason stopped in his tracks. "What can I do for you?"

"I wanted to let you know that early this morning, Buffalo narcotics police officer Jason Moore was killed at his safe house. Shot to the head."

Assassin style.

Chills racked Mason's body. Even in the summer night's warmth.

How many other assassins were out there?

Mason gritted his teeth. "When did this happen?"

"Around midnight. Deputy US Marshal Georgia Caballero from our northern district was shot in the process of protecting him, but the assailant got away. Fled the scene on foot. We have K-9s searching. We found their abandoned vehicle down the road."

Mason fingered the file he still held. "Any dossiers in it?"

"Yes, why?"

"Because someone tried to kill my witness, too, around the same time. They sent two assassins, but we took both out. We found a file in their vehicle with their pictures and information."

The man cussed. "I also heard they found Lincoln Luther dead. Suicide."

"Yes. Looks like this may be over."

A ding came through the phone. "Just a sec." Silence. "Just received confirmation that Buffalo PD is calling Lincoln's death a suicide for sure. Evidence points to him jumping from his window. We can all breathe a sigh of relief."

Could they? "I'll wait for your coroner's office to verify before celebrating."

"Probably not a bad idea. I'll keep you apprised of any updates. Stay safe."

"You, too." Mason walked back to Nash and relayed the information. "I'm not quite ready to relax. Not until I hear from—" His cell buzzed, and he glanced at the screen. "Dad, was just talking about you."

"Buffalo PD is saying their evidence is solid that Lincoln committed suicide, and hopefully an autopsy supports their findings."

"Agree." He told him about his conversation with Deputy Rollins. "Shame about Officer Moore. Emma said he was an outstanding policeman."

"I'm calling Nash back to the station. I'm pretty sure the threat is over."

"Do you really think that?"

"We'll find out at 2:00 p.m."

"Why? What's happening then?" He waved to Nash and headed back to the house.

"Layla and Lance Luther have called a joint press conference. I'm guessing to give news of their father's death."

"Okay, I'm heading back to Emma. We'll watch. Call me after." He stopped. "Dad, why would the assassins have business cards from both Darlene and Tom in their truck?"

"No idea, but I just interrogated Tom and asked that question. He confessed they are dating but doesn't know why the assassin had his card. Claims he's not the leak and doesn't know Darlene's whereabouts."

"Okay, thanks. Talk later." Mason ended the call and rubbed his neck.

He couldn't let down his guard. Not until he confirmed Emma and Sierra were safe.

Emma leaned forward on the couch to get a better view of Lance and Layla Luther later that afternoon. They had just walked to the podium outside Luther Shipping. The sun reflected off Layla's large diamond necklace. Dressed in a summer coral blazer and skirt, she had her straight, dark hair pulled into a bun at the nape of her neck. A sharp contrast to her brother's sandy-blond curls. They stood side by side in obvious harmony in what they were about to share with the world. Clearly, Lance had gotten back across the border without difficulties.

A camera zoomed in on the pair just as Lance took Layla's hand. She flinched but stayed by his side.

"Did you catch that?" Emma asked Mason. "She cringed at his touch."

"Why would that be?"

"These two have never gotten along, so I'm surprised Lance would even hold her hand. From everything I've read about the brother and sister, they fought like cats and dogs."

The caption across the TV screen read, "Luthers speak out about their father's organization."

Lance stepped up to the microphone and cleared his throat. "Thank you for attending our press conference. Layla and I have news to share." He raised their joined hands in the air. "We are here in unity. Together, we wanted to tell you our father took his life today." He stopped, his lip quivering.

Layla wiped away a tear and took his place at the podium. "What my brother is trying to say is, Lincoln Luther felt compelled to leave this world. He claimed to be a changed man and knew he couldn't live with himself after all the crimes he committed."

Audible murmurs sounded through the crowd gathered on the steps.

Layla pounded on the wooden stand. "Can I have your attention?" She waited for silence. "We're also here to tell you two things. One, we're selling Luther Shipping. Rest assured, we will compensate every employee."

Lance stepped closer to the microphone, inching Layla aside.

Once again, she flinched.

"They hate each other, don't they?" Mason asked.

"I'd say."

"The second item is to tell you Layla and I are launching a full investigation into the competency of the Buffalo PD and the Canadian Federal Police force. We're suing both departments."

Mason bolted off the couch. "What?"

The crowd whispered among themselves.

Layla raised her hands and hushed the reporters. "These two organizations failed to give our father a fair trial, and they will pay. *Dearly.*"

Her emphasis on the word *dearly* sent a tingle through Emma.

Lance looked straight into the camera, waggling his finger. "We're coming for you. You can't hide."

"What does that mean?" Emma inhaled sharply.

Layla nudged her brother aside. "What my brother is trying to say is we will leave no stone unturned to get a conviction into our father's wrongful incarceration. That's all we wanted to say."

"She's obviously the peacemaker of the two," Mason said.

A reporter moved forward. "Miss Luther, tell us why you're looking to sue the joint forces that took your father down. What do you have to gain?"

"Simple. Justice."

"But isn't it true you never got along with your father?" the man asked.

Her eyes flashed. "He was still my father and deserves justice."

A female reporter stuck her microphone out. "We've heard chatter that your father put a hit out on that same task force. Is that true?"

Lance stepped back to the podium. "I can answer that. A rogue employee put that hit out. Our lawyer, Will Gowland. We have had it removed from the dark web."

Emma snapped her gaze to Mason. "Is that true?"

"Dad said he was looking into it."

"Why didn't you tell me?"

Mason sat back down beside her. "I didn't want to get your hopes up."

"That's it for questions, folks," Layla said. "We'd ask you respect our family's privacy at this time of grief. Thank you." She grabbed her brother's hand and walked back into the building.

Seconds later, Mason's cell buzzed. "It's Dad. I'll put him on speaker." He punched the button. "I'm here with Emma. Did you watch the conference?"

"Yes. The nerve of them launching an investigation."

"Seth, are we finally safe?" Emma asked.

"Yes. What Lance said is true—the hit is down from the web. I checked before I called. You can voluntarily withdraw from the WPP if you want to leave the program. Do you?"

Tears welled in Emma's eyes. Was this real? Finally, this madness was over? "Yes, please."

"Okay, I'll start the process. Mason, I need all the manpower I can get right now to help with this supposed police conspiracy. I'm pulling Emma's protection detail. Stay close to her for now."

"Agreed."

Emma stood, wringing her hands together. "Does that mean I can go see my father?"

"Yes. I'm sorry to hear of his condition." Seth's gruff voice revealed his emotion. "Praying for your family. Gotta run. Stay in touch."

"Thank you." She turned to Mason after he disconnected the call. "I'm going to go get Sierra and our things. Can you drive us to the hospital?"

He smiled. "Of course."

An hour later, they walked through the entrance of the hospital where her father would spend his final moments on earth. Trepidation coursed through her limbs at the thought of losing him forever, but she also felt thankful she was able to say goodbye in person. She only hoped she wasn't too late.

Sierra bounced at her side as they reached the palliative floor.

Mason followed, keeping his ever-protective eyes peeled for any trouble. Seemed he didn't totally trust the Luthers were speaking the truth.

Not that she blamed him. And she appreciated his watch over Sierra.

Emma shifted her backpack and stepped up to the nurses' station. "I'm here to see Paul Williams. Can you point us to his room?"

"Are you family?"

"I'm his daughter Emma James."

"Let me check the list." She typed on the keyboard. "I don't see your name."

"Emma?" Her mother stood outside a room farther down the corridor. The frail, ashen-faced woman rushed toward the desk.

"Mom!" Emma flew into Daphne Williams's arms. "I'm here. Finally."

"God answered my prayer. Your father doesn't have long now."

Sneakers squeaked on the floor and caught Emma's attention. Her heart rate elevating, she pulled back from her mother's embrace.

"Emma girl!"

She let out the breath she'd been holding. Her sister.

Holly Williams flung her arms around her. "I thought I heard your voice. How come you're here?"

Sierra hugged her grandmother's legs. "Ammie!"

Her mother lifted the four-year-old. "I've missed you, sweet one."

Mason approached. "How about we take the

conversation into your dad's room? Too many listening ears."

Holly's eyes widened. "Why is Brady's brother here?"

Emma looped her arm through her sister's. "We'll explain everything in a minute. I need to see Dad first."

They walked into her father's room. Even though it was a hospital, the peaceful atmosphere surprised Emma. Gaither music played softly in the corner. Her dad's favorite.

Emma stepped to the foot of her father's bed. Tears threatened to fall at the sight of the frail man. *Lord, can You help him? Please.* She took a breath and walked to his side, gathering his hand in hers. "Papa, I'm here."

His eyes opened. "Em?"

Her mother cried behind her. "That's the first thing he's said in days."

Was her father waiting to see his youngest daughter before leaving earth?

She leaned down and kissed his cheek. "Yes, Papa. It's me."

"What took you so long?" His question came out in a ragged whisper.

Her father. Always the kidder.

"I had to stop and buy new shoes."

A joke they'd shared over the amount of footwear Emma had in her closet.

"Time for me to go." His faint, whispered words hushed the room.

"No, Papa. I asked Jesus to take care of you."

He closed his eyes. "He already has."

The heart monitor beeped a flat line.

Emma hugged the man who'd been everything to her and sobbed.

Lord, how much more will You take from me?

FIFTEEN

Mason backed out of the room to give the Williams family privacy and time to start the grieving process. He longed to take Emma in his arms to comfort her, but he knew her sister had an issue with his presence. Instead, he walked to the end of the hall and sat in a waiting chair. He checked his cell phone for updates, but so far, there were none. Other than his dad stating they still hadn't found Darlene. Her disappearance was a mystery to everyone.

The nurse hustled into Paul Williams's room after calling for a doctor. They would contact the funeral director to pick up the man's body.

God, why allow Your people to suffer?

Emma had lost so much in her life. The need to shield her from all the hurt bulldozed him. However, with the threat over, would she still want him around? So much had happened between them, he was at a loss for what their relationship looked like. Friends? Family? Of course, his heart told him he wanted more, but his head told him it was impossible.

The family walked out of the room and headed toward him.

Holly rushed at him, waggling her finger in his face. "Tell me why you're here."

He stood.

Her narrowed eyes spoke volumes. She disliked him.

Emma pulled her back. "Holly, it's okay. I know you were upset with him for not being around for me and Sierra after Brady died. That's in the past. Let me explain why he's here now. I'll give you the abridged version, and I can tell you more later."

She spent the next five minutes explaining the need to go into the WPP and how Mason had been assigned to protect her from the Luthers. "Don't blame him."

Holly's mouth dropped. "It's hard not to as I know the hurt you went through."

Emma grasped Holly's shoulders. "It's time to let that go and forgive him."

He raised his hands. "I'm sorry, Holly. I take full responsibility. I should have been there after Brady died."

Holly bit her lip and nodded. "Thank you for being there for them now."

"No worries." His cell phone buzzed, and he checked the screen. "It's my father." He stepped away and answered. "What's up, Dad?"

"Get out of there. Now."

He pivoted, his pulse rising. "Why? What's going on?"

Emma's eyes widened.

She obviously caught the alarm in his voice.

Not again, God.

"Deputy Rollins called me, as you weren't answering your phone. One of his other witnesses was just taken out. Katrina Arnold. The threat isn't over. Get Emma and Sierra back to Chuck's. Nash is headed there now. I've alerted hospital security. They're on their way to protect her family."

"Is it safe to go to the B&B?"

"It's the only place left to go. I'll let Chuck know you're coming. Hurry!" He clicked off.

Mason grabbed Emma's arm. "Em, we need to go."

"What's happened?" she asked.

"The threat isn't over." He would explain about Deputy Rollins's call later, but his first priority right now was keeping her and Sierra out of harm's way. "I'm sorry. We need to move."

Her lip quivered, and she pointed to her family. "Will they be safe?"

"Security is on their way to this floor," he said. "They will help."

Daphne pulled her daughter into her arms. "Emma, go. We're fine."

Holly embraced the pair. "Stay safe."

"I love you, both. I'll get in touch when this is really over." Emma pulled away and lifted Sierra. "Time to go, Sisi."

The quaver in her voice was undeniable.

Mason clamped his jaw, his entire body tensing

at the thought they were still in danger. This had to end. Once and for all.

When they reached the entrance, he instructed them to hold back while he checked the surroundings. He stepped outside, the heat of the day slamming him like a hot oven. He rested his hand on his sidearm and glanced around. Nothing seemed out of place. He motioned for them to come, and they ran to the sedan Chuck had provided.

He started the car and screeched out of the parking lot. "I'm taking the back roads in case we're followed."

Mason pulled into traffic, keeping a close watch in the rearview mirror. So far, he didn't spot a tail. He wove in and out of the lanes to pass slower-moving cars. He needed to get them out of the city. Fast.

Five minutes later, he turned onto a country road. The highway's solitude sent relief coursing through his veins.

Emma gripped the console. "How could this have happened, Mason? I thought they took the hit down."

Had the Luthers' press conference just been an elaborate hoax to get them to relax their guard on all the witnesses?

That had to be the answer, but the question remained.

Who was really behind everything?

The car lurched forward and sputtered.

He stepped on the gas, but instead of speeding up, the sedan slowed.

The engine was dying.

"What's happening?" Emma asked.

Sierra cried in the back seat.

Mason pulled to the side of the road just as the car breathed its last breath.

Had someone sabotaged the vehicle? They were easy targets out in the open.

And had nowhere to run.

"Stay here," he said. "I'm calling Dad. We need to get someone here fast."

He stepped outside and pulled out his phone.

No service.

Impossible. They weren't that far out in the country. He spotted cell towers in the distance. Had someone jammed their signal?

Anything was possible, and with the Luthers' clout, it didn't surprise him. Earlier thoughts about their press statements being a ploy popped into his mind again. He glanced in both directions, looking for a place to hide them until he could call for help. Mason didn't like the open area. He checked his phone again.

No service.

God, why are You allowing this? Emma is one of Your own.

He wiped his clammy palms on his jeans as his lunch turned to lead in his stomach. Past fears of not protecting those he loved surfaced. First his mother. Now Emma and Sierra. How can he save them from what his gut was telling him was about to happen?

Think, Mason. Think. God, will You show me how to save them?

He turned and glanced in the opposite direction.

An abandoned silo in the distance caught his attention. It was a bit of a walk, but a good place to hide. Until reinforcements arrived.

He hurried to the car and opened Emma's door. "My phone isn't working," he whispered. "I believe they're jamming our signal. We need to walk to the silo down the road and take cover."

Her face turned ashen, her eyes widening.

"Em, I know this is scary. But I can't have us sitting out here in the open." He glanced at Sierra in the back seat. "It's not safe."

Emma brushed her bangs aside, her fingers shaking. "This was supposed to be over."

"I know. I'm now wondering if the conference was just a ploy for us to take our guard down." How could he have been so blind to their tactics? "Unfortunately, it worked. They killed a witness in WITSEC."

"Who?"

"US border officer Katrina Arnold."

Emma's lip trembled. "She was engaged to be married this fall."

"I'm so sorry. We need to move." He opened the back door, grabbed Jerome and lifted Sierra out. "Time for a little walk, Sisi. Wanna play hide-and-seek?"

"Yes, Y'ncle Mason!" She squirmed in his arms. "Down, please."

He walked to the side of the road, set Sierra down and handed her the giraffe. Her bright green eyes smiled at him, tugging at his heart. A lump clogged his throat and he swallowed. He must protect this little one at all costs. "Wait here first. Okay, Sisi?"

She nodded.

Emma joined them, her shoulders drooping.

He knew she was sick and tired of running. He didn't blame her. The Luthers—or whoever was doing this—were relentless.

An engine revving sounded in the distance.

He glanced eastward.

An SUV approached at high speed, careening toward them. "Emma, get Sierra behind the back tires and stay low!" Mason whipped out his weapon and crouched behind the other wheel. *You failed again.*

He was too late in getting them to safety.

Emma grabbed Sierra and squatted on the ground in front of the rear rim with her back leaning against the tire. Her pulse hammered as she clung to her weeping daughter. *Lord, protect us!* Somehow the Luthers had still tracked their location. Or had someone bugged Mason's phone?

A thought emerged. "Mason, is your cell phone's GPS turned on?"

"I've kept it off for weeks now. They're not using my phone to find us." He held his gun tight against his chest.

The vehicle's engine sounded closer. The perpetrators were almost here.

They were out of time.

Sierra cried.

Emma gripped the four-year-old closer. "I've got you, baby girl." Her words fell flat in her own mind. *You have nothing right now. You're holding on by a thread.*

Screeching tires drew her attention from her stupor.

She held her breath.

Shots rang out, and bullets pummeled the vehicle. Windows shattered, pieces of glass showering the pavement.

She curled herself and Sierra into an even tighter ball, praying the tires would protect them.

Mason hit his magazine release and looked at the bullets before slamming it back into his gun. "Whatever happens, stay down."

"What are you going to do?"

"I need to take a shot." He turned and peeked over the car. "They're getting out of the vehicle."

Emma clamped her eyes shut and silently pleaded with God to keep them safe.

Mason fired.

The sound boomed in her ears, and she cringed after each shot. She wished she'd brought the Glock that Seth had given her, but she refused to scare Sierra further, especially when they thought the threat was over.

The assailants returned fire, peppering the vehicle.

She opened her eyes and prayed once again for help.

Another shot rang out.

Mason howled, and his gun flew in her direction, clattering on the pavement. He held his arm, his chest rising and falling in quick syncopation. His face contorted.

A red spot grew on his shirt, and Emma sucked in a sharp breath. "You've been shot."

She needed to help before the situation worsened. "Sisi, I'm going to put you down. Curl into a ball and don't move."

Her daughter obeyed. Jerome slipped from Sierra's hand, falling just out of her reach.

Emma grabbed Mason's gun and fired three shots.

Click.

She pulled the trigger again.

Click.

They were out of ammo.

Another car approached and squealed to a stop nearby. Pounding footsteps told her more assailants had arrived.

"Stop. Police."

Emma eased her head up.

Darlene crouched behind her open cruiser door, her gun raised. How had she found them?

Another round of gunfire erupted. Exploding glass showered the pavement.

Darlene fired again.

The masked assailants hopped back into their vehicle and sped off.

Emma scrambled over to Mason, her hands trembling as she choked back the tears threatening to fall. "Mason! Let me see where you were hit." She glanced at the pool of red beside him.

His ashen face told her extreme pain tormented his body, and he would probably lose consciousness soon.

"How did—"

"Shh. Don't talk. You need to save your energy." She removed her summer cardigan and wrapped it around the wound. "We have to get you to the hospital."

"No, they'll find us."

Darlene's footsteps alerted Emma to the female cop's presence. The question remained—was she working for the Luthers?

Emma stood and braced herself in a defensive stance. She would not be taken down lightly.

Then again, why shoot at the masked men if she wasn't on their side?

Nevertheless, Emma did not trust this woman.

"You okay?" Darlene asked, holstering her weapon.

"Mason has been shot, and we're out of bullets." Emma raised the gun.

"Here, in case you need more." Darlene pulled a clip from her vest and tossed it over.

Emma loaded it into Mason's nine-millimeter and stuffed it in the back of her waistband. She then flew at the constable and grabbed her by the collar. "Where have you been and how did you know where to find us?"

"Calm down, Emma." She pulled her hands away. "I can explain later. Let's get Mason into my cruiser. Stat. You need to trust me."

She was right. Emma had no choice but to comply. "Can you handle him? I'll get Sierra."

Darlene nodded.

Emma picked up her crying daughter, who remained curled in her ball. "Good girl, Sisi. Time to go." She scooped up Jerome from the pavement.

Darlene scrambled over to Mason. "Buddy, I need to get you in my car. Can you stand?"

"Where. Have. You. Been?" Mason's jarred words asked Darlene the same question Emma wanted answered.

The female constable grabbed under his strong arm and helped him to his feet. "Let's get you to safety."

The pair shuffled over to the cruiser. Darlene put Mason in the back seat.

Emma and Sierra followed. "Baby girl, I'm going to put you beside Uncle Mason. Can you keep him company?"

Sierra crawled in beside him. "Y'ncle Mason. You sick?"

His lips curled upward slightly. "I'm okay, Sisi."

Sierra leaned against him like a kitten taking refuge beside her mother.

Emma fastened her daughter's seat belt and jumped in the front seat.

Darlene started the ignition.

Emma grabbed her arm. "Tell us where you've been. Now!"

The woman faced Emma. "Layla Luther called me all upset, stating someone was out to kill her. She wanted my help."

"Why would she call you?" Mason's weakened voice revealed his condition.

"I have a picture of you with her and Lance at a fund-raiser," Emma said. "How do you know them?"

Darlene bit her lip. "Long story, but to make it quick, I discovered Layla and I had something in common—we were both abused as young girls. My father would sneak into my room late at night when I was seven. It continued into my teenage years." She gripped the steering wheel tighter. "The same happened with Layla's father. That's why she started Layla's Centre of Hope.

She wanted to provide shelter for abused women. A place to hide."

"So you felt you had a camaraderie with her?" Emma asked.

"Yes. She's a good person. I invested in her foundation, so I went to the fundraiser."

"Okay, but why have you been MIA the past few days?" Emma still didn't trust her story. It made little sense.

"As I mentioned, Layla called in a panic and wanted protection."

"But why not contact the Buffalo PD? Why you?" She wasn't buying this woman's tale. "Darlene, this doesn't add up. Be honest."

Darlene blew out a long breath. "I am. Layla doesn't trust any of the Buffalo PD. Most are on her father's payroll. We're friends, and she trusts me."

Mason leaned forward. "Why not go to Lance for help?"

"That spoiled brat? He's useless." Darlene's tone conveyed her dislike for the brother.

"Okay, but why not tell my father? Why disappear?"

"Do you need to ask? Your father would not understand." The constable's gaze moved to Sierra. "Not when it comes to his Tiddlywinks."

That part was true. Seth James would do anything for his granddaughter. Even distrust any suspicious activity, and this certainly fell into that category.

"I returned from Buffalo after the hit was removed and have been following you from a distance. Just to be sure you were safe." Darlene's cell phone buzzed.

Wait. Hadn't the suspects jammed the signal?

Emma turned and glanced at Mason, chewing on her lip. Would he get her question in his dazed state?

His eyes narrowed, and he shook his head.

He wasn't buying his partner's story, either.

Darlene glanced at her phone. "I need to take this call in private. I'll be right back." She got out and walked to where their bullet-riddled vehicle sat.

Her muffled voice rose, and her expression told Emma she was arguing with someone. Darlene glanced back at the cruiser.

Something wasn't right.

"Drive, Em." Mason's weakened whisper held urgency. "Don't. Trust. Her."

Emma ensured Darlene had once again averted her gaze before crawling over the console and into the driver's seat. She eased the gear into Drive and stepped on the gas.

The tires screeched.

Emma looked in the rearview mirror.

Darlene ran after them, waving her hands in the air.

She accelerated, wanting to get away from the suspicious constable. "Where to, Mason?"

"Here, check my cell." He dropped his phone over the seat.

She kept her eyes on the road and fumbled for the phone. She glanced at the screen.

Three cell bars.

"It's working now." She peeked back at Mason.

He grappled with his belt and tied it around his arm. "Jeff's fishing cabin. Head to Niagara-on-the-Lake. I'll tell you where to turn." His breath sounded labored. "Ask Jeff to meet us there and Dad, too. Need to rest and—"

He slumped back in the seat.

"Mason, don't pass out on me now."

Lord, help me.

Emma clicked on Mason's contacts, found Jeff's number and hit the dial button.

"Mason, buddy. How are you?"

"Jeff, it's Emma. Mason's been shot in the upper arm." Her words came out breathless. *Calm down, girl.* She inhaled and exhaled slowly.

"What? Where are you?"

"On our way to your fishing cabin. Mason wants you to meet us there. He just passed out."

"Get him to a hospital."

"I can't. Not safe." How could she convince this man they needed his medical expertise? "Mason trusts you, Jeff. Can you help? Please. I don't know what else to do."

A loud sigh passed through the phone. "I'm about an hour out. I'll gather supplies and be on my way."

"Thank you." She hung up and dialed Seth.

"Emma, Darlene just called and said you stole her cruiser."

"Mason and I don't trust her story. It's too full of holes."

She turned onto a back road she knew would take them to their destination. The secondary highway was in a densely wooded area and would provide cover.

"Agreed. Where are you?"

"We're headed to Jeff's fishing—"

The cell phone beeped, and the call dropped.

"No!" She glanced at the screen.

No battery.

She'd just lost her contact with the outside world.

They were on their own.

SIXTEEN

Mason swallowed, hoping to lubricate his parched mouth. Where was he? What happened? A rocking motion told him he was in a moving car. Sharp, piercing pain jabbed his arm and resonated throughout his body. The gunshot. He opened his eyes and sat upright, grimacing.

"Mason. Stay still." Emma's hushed voice commanded obedience.

He leaned back and glanced at the four-year-old beside him. She snuggled into him and slept soundly. Her light snoring sent a wave of peace through his nervous demeanor.

"Where are we?" he asked.

"Niagara-on-the-Lake, driving around. I wanted to put her to sleep, and you passed out before telling me where Jeff's cabin is located." She raised his cell phone. "Your cell died. How are you feeling?"

"Tired." He rubbed his foggy eyes and glanced out the window to get his bearings. "Okay, I know where we are. The cabin is about ten minutes from here. Take your next left and then right onto road 87." His heart palpitated. "In case I pass out again from the pain, look for a wooden sign with a fish on top. You can't miss it. The dirt driveway will take you down to his lake cabin. Is he coming?"

"Yes."

"And Dad?"

"The call dropped before I could tell him. Is he aware of Jeff's cabin?"

Mason leaned his head back. "No. Jeff bought this place when Dad and I weren't communicating."

Mason, how could you have been so selfish and not tried harder to mend your broken relationship?

Now they would pay the price for Mason's mistake.

Twelve minutes later, he spotted Jeff's ugly fish ahead. "There it is, Em." He pointed and then plopped his arm back down. The blood loss and pain weakened his body. He prayed he'd be able to walk to the log cabin deep into the woods.

She turned right.

The car jostled on a bumpy dirt road.

"Whoa. Why isn't his driveway paved?" Emma asked.

"Good question." He winced each time the tires hit a pothole.

"Mason, how do we get in? I don't want to have to wait in the car."

"I know where there's a key. Park and I'll show you."

Emma pulled the car close to the front cabin entrance and turned off the ignition. "Wait there.

Let me help you." She scrambled out, eased him from the seat and wrapped her arm around his waist. "Let's go slow."

Mason glanced at the log cabin set among a densely wooded area at the lake's edge. A docked boat rocked on the choppy waters, banging against the pier. The wind had picked up, and the setting sun kissed the horizon, sending a beautiful display of color in the sky and mirroring it on the glistening lake.

They headed to the cabin's porch. He pointed to the railing. "See the wood knot? It's a hidden compartment. The key is in there."

Emma rubbed her fingers along the wood and clicked the knot. The secret hole popped open. "Cool trick. I'm shocked you'd let him leave a key out in the open, though."

"Jeff is stubborn but, in this case, a lifesaver." He stumbled, his weakened legs almost giving out, and he grabbed the railing.

Emma tightened her grip. "You okay?"

"Losing strength. Open the door."

She helped him up the stairs and unlocked the cabin.

"I've got it from here. Go get Sierra." He staggered into the living room area, then, cradling his left arm, inched over to the couch and eased down on it. His mind returned to the conversation with Darlene in the car. Could they trust the reason for her sudden disappearance, or was she the leak?

Emma returned carrying a sleeping Sierra, interrupting the questions racing through his mind.

"Wow, the excitement and the drive must have tuckered her out." Mason pointed to the door at the foot of the stairs. "You can take her to the master bedroom. It's amazing and has a deck with a lake view."

"I'm not sure how much longer she'll sleep. Be right back." Emma entered the room and returned quickly.

A car engine sounded.

She walked to the window. "Jeff's here. Thank You, God."

Moments later, the door burst open, and Jeff appeared carrying his medical bag and a cooler. "How's our patient?" He rushed forward and dropped beside Mason. "Buddy, stay still. I need to inspect your wound." Jeff removed the sweater Emma had wrapped around his arm. "It appears the bullet passed through. You've lost some blood. I brought your type, so I'm going to get more into your veins."

Ten minutes later, Jeff had Mason set up with an IV to pump additional blood into him and promised he'd feel better soon.

Hopefully. Because Mason needed to protect the girls.

"Emma, can you get me a granola bar from the far right cupboard?" Jeff asked.

She went to the kitchen and returned. "It appears this is the only food you have, Jeff." She unwrapped the bar and gave it to Mason.

"I haven't been here in a couple of weeks. There's a small grocery store nearby." He stood and walked to the door. "He'll need more than that, so I'll be back with food. Don't venture far off. A storm is brewing, and these parts are known for flooding." He left the cabin.

"Great, that's all we need." Emma peeked out the window. "Thank God Jeff came prepared. I'm going to lie down with Sierra. You rest."

Hours later, Mason woke to rain pinging off the tin roof. Darkness had fallen. He glanced at his watch. Two a.m. He wiped the perspiration from his forehead. "Emma? Jeff? Where are you?"

Movement sounded from the bedroom, and the door opened. Emma stepped into the living room, rubbing her eyes. "What is it?"

"Where's Jeff?"

"I must have fallen asleep. He's not back?" She walked to the window and glanced out. "His car isn't here. It's raining pretty hard."

He pointed to the end table. "Check the radio for weather reports."

She snapped the lamp and radio on.

"This just in," the DJ announced. "There are reports of flooding and trees blocking roads in the Niagara-on-the-Lake area. Crews are working hard to clear them."

"Poor Jeff. He says this happens a lot here.

Come sit." He bunched his legs up and patted the cushion beside him. "How are you?"

Emma sat. "Confused. Tired. Angry."

"Understand. This has been tough on you. I'm sorry I haven't been able to catch whoever is doing this. I've failed you."

"Are you kidding?" She moved closer. "You've been our rock, Mason. I shudder to think of what I would have done if you hadn't showed up to protect us." She caressed his face. "You've given me strength to fight."

"How? All I've done is fumble at every turn. Just ask Dad. I'm sure that's what he'd say."

She took his right hand in hers. "Mason, you need to forgive your father. Forgive yourself. Your mother's death was not his fault and certainly not yours. Come back to God."

He recoiled at her words. "You don't understand how it feels to not live up to someone's standards. To live with guilt, knowing if you'd done something different, your loved one may still be alive today."

Her eyes narrowed and she jumped up. "How can you even say that? I've lived with the guilt of Brady's death for three long years. Don't you get it? Your brother would still be alive if I hadn't gotten so angry that night."

He eased himself into a seated position, ignoring the pain stabbing his arm. "Em, you need to live by your own words. Brady's death wasn't your fault, and he wouldn't want you to carry the guilt any longer. The truck driver fell asleep at the wheel."

She paced the room, running her fingers through her long red hair. "I yelled at him. I was just so tired. Tired of a colicky child. Tired of his long hours at the station. Tired of…" Her hand flew to her mouth.

"What?"

She went back to the couch and scooched beside him. "He loved you deeply, you know."

Could he tell her the harsh words he'd said to Brady just before the accident? Words Mason would take back in a heartbeat if he'd only known they would be his last?

He tucked a stray curl behind her ear. "I need to tell you something." He averted his gaze.

She guided his chin back to look her in the face. "Tell me."

"I never blamed myself for Brady's death, but I said some things just before the accident I shouldn't have."

She took a sharp inhale. "What?"

"Brady called after you had your fight and explained what happened. I told him to pull up his britches and move on because his life was perfect. He had no reason to complain. He had a beautiful wife and a sweet daughter." Mason clenched his jaw. "I yelled at him. Those were the last words I said to my brother before he died, and I couldn't take them back…"

She gathered him into an embrace. "Seems like we both need to forgive ourselves for many things. It's time to move on."

What was she saying? Move on with whom?

He pulled back and studied her face. "Time for what, Em?"

"Time to come back to God. Brady told me you made a decision for Christ when you were younger. He has a purpose for you. Just ask Him what it is."

Not what he'd hoped she'd say. Could he pour out his heart? Or would she crush it like Zoe did? He took a breath. It *was* time. "What if I told you I want you in my life? You and Sierra."

Her face was so close to him. Her lips within reach. He leaned closer.

She bolted off the couch. "I can't."

"Why, Em?"

She pivoted. "You don't know the truth about your brother."

"What are you talking about?"

She sat back down and took his hands in hers. "I need to be honest with you about Brady. Something I've never told anyone, because no one would have believed me."

He waited, holding his breath.

"Brady…" She bit her lip. "Brady hit me. Multiple times."

Mason gasped and pulled back. "You must be wrong. He would never have done that."

"I'm not. Do you remember the time you visited me in the hospital shortly after I had Sierra?"

"Yes, you fell down the stairs."

"That was a lie Brady concocted. He pushed me, Mason." Tears rolled down her cheeks. "He almost killed me. All over a burned supper. One night he choked me."

"No! He. Wouldn't. Do. That." How could she blame Brady for this horrific act? His brother had been a cop. A good one. Had she messed with his brother's mind like Zoe messed with his?

Mason tried to stand but fell back down on the couch.

Emma reached for him. "I'm sorry."

He swatted her hand away. "I need to be alone."

Emma hurried to the kitchen, hoping to find something sweet to boost her weary body and get away from the upsetting conversation with Mason. She'd known he wouldn't believe her about Brady, especially after his trust in women had faltered after Zoe swindled him out of his life's savings.

However, being so close to Mason solidified how she felt about him. When he almost kissed her—twice—she knew her feelings had gone too far. She couldn't risk the misery again, but she wanted to tell him the truth if she had any hope of a relationship with the man who'd stolen her heart.

But could she trust someone who reminded her

of Brady? Sierra would never recover from another loss in her life.

He's not like his brother. The thought raced into her mind. It didn't matter now. He didn't believe her.

Emma grabbed the one lone juice box from Jeff's fridge and headed back to check on her daughter.

She opened the door and stepped inside, dropping the juice.

The bed was empty.

She searched the room and stepped onto the patio. She shivered from the damp night, the breeze assaulting her body. "Sierra! Where are you?" The now-black clouds promised more rain.

Her gaze darted left, then right. Panic roared through her. Her daughter was out there somewhere in the dark. Alone. In the woods among wild animals.

Her heartbeat galloped and weakened her limbs. She grabbed the patio railing to steady herself. *Lord, help me find Sierra.*

She moved back into the living room and stopped.

Mason was passed out on the couch, his face even whiter than before. Had her news sent him into a relapse? She shook Mason. "Wake up! I need you."

Nothing.

Emma glanced around the room. She eyed a

bulky man's jacket on the coatrack and pulled it down, slipping it on. Emma took Mason's weapon from her waistband and stuffed the nine-millimeter into the coat's pocket. Rummaging through the kitchen drawers, she found multiple different-size flashlights and grabbed a large one. She needed to prepare for a search in the woods. Just in case she stumbled upon wild animals or worse...

What if someone had kidnapped her daughter?

Maybe Sierra had simply gone exploring.

Her gut told her that wasn't true.

Emma found paper and scratched a quick note for Mason and Jeff, praying they would find her message.

She stepped out into the murky night and turned on the flashlight. The wind oscillated her curls as raindrops splattered over the deck. She pulled the large hood on, smothering her head, and ascended the porch stairs. Emma knew she must move quickly in case another thunderstorm hit. Sierra would be hysterical if that happened. The storms had pummeled Ontario the past week.

She shone the beam around the woods, spotting a structure in the distance. Had Sierra gone in search of another adventure? Her daughter's overactive imagination found fun in almost anything.

Emma ran toward the building, branches slapping her face. She ignored the sharp pain and kept moving.

A noise stopped her in her tracks.

Sierra cried somewhere close.

"Baby girl! Where are you?" she yelled.

Emma pulled her hood off and listened closely. Her daughter's muffled cries intensified. Behind her.

She pivoted and dashed toward her daughter's sobs. "Sierra, call out to Mama."

The noise heightened.

Emma moved toward the sound. Seconds later, she found her daughter sitting against an enormous oak tree. Emma bolted to Sierra and fell beside her. "Baby girl, I'm here. You're okay. Why did you leave without telling me?" She pulled Sierra into her arms.

It was then she noticed her daughter's hands were tied behind her back. Frost chilled Emma's veins, turning them to ice.

Branches snapped behind her, but it was too late.

A blunt object whacked against her head, blindsiding and thrusting her into darkness.

Emma woke to a rocking sensation, pain thrashing in her head. She rubbed the bump. Where was she? An image of Sierra crying by a tree formed in her dazed mind. Then the awareness of something exploding on her head surfaced. Sierra? Emma bolted upright and immediately regretted the movement. Nausea rose as the room swam in her vision. She held her head and breathed in and out slowly, waiting for it to pass. *Lord, please help*

Sierra be okay and Mason to forgive me. She now couldn't fathom being without him. Not after everything they've been through and the feelings she now knew were solid.

She loved him.

She just prayed he would believe her about his brother. The news would also get out to his father. The idea of having to tell Seth James the son he bragged about at every turn had had an angry streak scared her. He'd be devastated. Could he realize Mason was the son who'd always been there, even when his father tried to push him away?

Father.

The conversation with her dad before he died resurfaced.

"I asked Jesus to take care of you."

He closed his eyes. "He already has."

Emma's heavenly Father took care of His children. She'd been angry at Him for allowing events to happen in her life. And thought she'd had everything figured out. A loving husband. A little girl. A nice house.

Only her perfect life was a facade.

The secret she'd kept for so long had rotted her love for God. She accused Him for allowing her twisty, tormented path in life. A path she pretended was flawless. She *was* a liar. Emma blamed all her sorrows on the One who held her close. She saw that now.

Tears spattered on her hands. Tears she hadn't realized flowed down her cheeks. She hung her head.

Lord, I'm sorry for blaming You. For not trusting You with all aspects of my life. I felt like You'd blindsided me and changed my path, when all along, You just steered me down a different one. Your path. I see that now. Please forgive me. I surrender my heart back to You. Use what's left of it for Your glory. I don't care what You do to me, but please save Sierra and Mason. I love You.

Peace enveloped her in a gigantic hug.

The nausea and dizziness passed.

Lightning flashed, and a clap of thunder boomed.

Emma jumped and glanced around the structure to determine her location. Fishy smells wafted in the air, assaulting her nose. *No!* Her captor had laid Emma on a cot in a boathouse. On the water.

Her childhood fear rose, and images of her almost drowning formed. *Lord, not water.*

Breathe.

The word popped in her mind. It must be from God. She obeyed and took several long inhales. Her rapid heartbeat slowed.

Emma glanced around the room, hoping to find her daughter.

Sierra slept on another cot. Thankfully, her daughter was unaware of the storm raging outside.

"It's about time you woke up."

Emma turned toward her captor's voice.

"Tracey?"

SEVENTEEN

Movement registered close to Mason as someone shouted his name. He wrestled with coming out of his unconscious state until a pungent odor bolted him awake. He opened his eyes and found Jeff hovering over him, waving smelling salts. Mason eased himself until a sharp pain punched him in the arm. He fell back down.

Jeff checked his bandage. "You must have passed out again. The bleeding has stopped, thankfully. I need you to eat. I'm making oatmeal."

"You get caught in the storm?"

"Yes, a downed tree blocked the road. Crews finally came." He rubbed a welt around his right eye. "Good thing, as when I tried to remove the mess, I got hit in the face. This is going to be a lovely color tomorrow."

An image swarmed in his mind. Emma with a bruised eye. She'd tried to hide the purple mess with makeup but was unsuccessful. Brady had told him she ran into the door.

Mason had believed his brother, but what if—
It can't be true.
But why would Emma lie?
Brady, how could you have done that to your

beautiful wife? Was his father aware? The news would crush him.

Mason eased himself back up. He wanted to talk to her. "Where's Emma?"

"I assume she's asleep."

"I need you to check. Please."

Jeff nodded and knocked to announce his presence. He waited a few seconds before entering. Moments later, he burst from the room, holding Jerome.

"They're both gone. I only found this in the bed." Jeff stopped at the end table near the door. "Wait." He held up a notepad. "It's from Emma. Says she's looking for Sierra."

Once again, Mason attempted to sit. "I need to find them. It's not safe."

Jeff pushed him back onto the couch. "Your body is still recovering."

"You don't understand. They've found us again."

"How?"

"Not sure."

Jeff stood. "At least eat a few bites. You can't help her if you're as weak as a kitten." He walked into the kitchen.

Mason placed his feet on the floor and sat leaning on his elbows. He buried his face in his hands.

His worst fears had come to fruition. He'd failed to protect the person he loved, but would she allow him in their lives after he refused to believe her about Brady?

Wait—what? The realization he was totally and deeply in love with Emma James hit him over the head. He wanted her and Sierra in his life. Permanently.

But how could he protect her?

"He that dwelleth in the secret place of the most High shall abide under the shadow of the Almighty. I will say of the Lord, He is my refuge and my fortress: my God; in him will I trust. Surely he shall deliver thee from the snare of the fowler, and from the noisome pestilence. He shall cover thee with his feathers, and under his wings shalt thou trust: his truth shall be thy shield and buckler."

Mason choked in a breath. The verses he'd memorized as a child popped back into his mind. *God, are You there? Are You telling me to give my life back to You and I'll be safe under Your wings?*

He couldn't have anything happen to Emma after his last harsh words. He needed to tell her he believed her and he was sorry. But first, he had to talk to God and ask for forgiveness. It wasn't God who betrayed him. Mason had betrayed and abandoned God.

Mason slowly rose and knelt in front of the couch. *God, I blamed You for so many things that have gone wrong in my life. I'm sorry. Please forgive my stupidity. I surrender back to You. My ultimate protector. Take my life.*

Tears streamed down his face.

"Buddy, you okay?" Jeff placed a bowl of oatmeal on the coffee table and knelt.

"Just giving my life back to God."

Jeff squeezed Mason's good shoulder. "So glad to hear it. Will you eat something now before racing—"

A hard knock sounded.

Mason bristled. It was the middle of the night, and their location was supposedly concealed. "Get me your rifle."

Seconds later, Jeff handed him the weapon. He raised it, but pain shot through his wounded arm, and he grimaced, lowering it again. *Lord, please give me strength against whoever is behind the door.*

"Mason, give it to me." Jeff held out his hand. "Open the door slowly."

He shuffled over and stood to the right of the door. "Ready?"

Jeff armed and raised the Remington rifle. "Go."

Mason flung open the door.

Jeff stepped forward. "Hold it there!"

Mason grabbed the intruder by his arm and flung him against the wall. "Who are you?"

"Deputy US Marshal Darryl Rollins. I'm looking for Constable Mason James." Rain dripped from the man's jacket, forming a puddle on the floor.

Mason held his good arm under the marshal's

chin, ignoring the pain coursing through his other arm. "That's me. How did you find us?"

"Your father. Let me go. I'm here to help."

"Wait. How did my father know where we are? My phone died before Emma told him."

Jeff lowered the rifle. "I called him, Mason. I was worried and thought you might need backup."

Smart thinking. "Good. Is he on his way, too?"

"Yes," Darryl said. "The storm hampered my trip from Buffalo, so I'm sure it also did your father's. Mason, you're choking me."

He released the marshal. "Try anything and Jeff will shoot."

Darryl raised his hands. "Understood."

Jeff moved beside the deputy and pointed to the coffee table. "Buddy, eat some oatmeal. Please."

Mason knew his friend wouldn't relent, so he sat and picked up the bowl. "Deputy, tell me why you're here."

"I know your mole's identity."

Mason almost dropped his spoon. "Who?"

"Tracey Smith."

"The *computer technician*?" Mason thought back to the number of times she'd been in their safe houses. Every one except for Chuck's bed-and-breakfast. Everything made sense. She'd supply them with their needs, medications, computer, and she knew their locations. Had she also poisoned Emma's insulin? "Wait. How do you know Tracey?"

"She's my sister."

Mason whistled. "What? Aren't you American?"

"Canadian by birth, but dual citizenship. We were born in the Niagara area, but our parents divorced when we were teens. Dad got a job in Buffalo and I chose to live with him. Tracey stayed with Mom."

"How do you know she's the leak?" Mason gulped down the rest of the oatmeal.

"When our witness locations in Buffalo were compromised, I suspected someone had hacked our WITSEC records but couldn't figure out who until you called to accuse me, since my prints were on the tracking device."

"Explain."

"After you called, I remembered something from a few weeks ago," Darryl told him. "I was visiting Tracey, and she confessed she thought her husband was cheating on her, so she asked me for the device. She wanted to track him. She's also good at hacking, so I put two and two together." He ran his fingers through his wet black hair. "I didn't want to believe she'd do such a thing, but it all adds up now. I came here because Tracey's husband, Jack, told me that was a lie. He wasn't cheating. The Luthers kidnapped their son and were holding him. They told them if Tracey didn't help, they'd kill Cody."

"Was it Lincoln?"

"Jack didn't know. They used a voice enhancer."

Mason stood. "Why did you come here?"

"Because Jack called in a frantic state and told me Tracey left the house saying your father would never forgive her for what she was about to do. A final task to get their son back. He pleaded with me to find her, so that's when I called your dad."

"Jeff, we need supplies. Do you have flashlights and another rifle?" Mason grabbed a coat from his friend's rack and put it on.

"You couldn't lift my Remington, Mason. You're too weak. How are you going to help Emma? Let me go with Deputy Rollins. You know I'm an excellent shot."

Darryl pulled a Glock from the back of his pants. "Use my backup."

Mason nodded. "Jeff, I need you to stay here in case Emma returns. Also, please get in touch with Dad. Tell him what's happened."

Jeff pulled flashlights from the kitchen drawer. "Here, take these. And stay safe. I'm praying."

"You, too." Mason accepted the lights, threw the jacket hood over his head and stepped out into the rainy night with Darryl at his heels.

The wind and rain assaulted him, but he kept moving through the woods.

Loud voices stopped him in his tracks. He raised his fisted hand, indicating Darryl should do the same.

He listened closely to isolate the direction of the sounds.

"That way!" Mason pointed. "There's a dock in that area. It has to be them. The rain should conceal our approach."

Darryl nodded, and they raced toward the sound. Mason prayed with every step he took.

Emma's muscles tensed at the sight of the computer technician sitting in the corner watching over them. The woman Emma had trusted had betrayed them all, and for what reason? Didn't she have what most women wanted? Husband. Child. Successful career. Emma bolted off the cot, ready to defend her daughter at all costs.

Tracey hopped up and raised a weapon in Sierra's direction. "Do not make me hurt your sweet daughter."

Emma folded her arms. "Why, Tracey? Why are you helping the Luthers?"

Tracey's lips quivered, and she stumbled backward. "They have Cody."

Emma's hand flew to her mouth. *"What?"*

"Yes. After the trial concluded, they contacted me and told me they were watching my son. Sent me pictures of him at school and said that if I didn't help them, they'd kidnap Cody. They wanted me to get information on the witnesses. I started out just giving them tidbits of data, trying to stall them." She paused. "Then, they took him a few weeks ago. Said I wasn't helping them enough and needed to step it up or my son would pay the price. They threatened to kill him if I didn't help them find the witness locations." She shut her eyes and blew out a breath. "I never wanted this, Emma. I wouldn't hurt a fly."

"Yet here you are, pointing a gun at my daughter." Would Emma do the same if the roles were reversed and they'd kidnapped Sierra?

Without a doubt. She would do *anything* to save her daughter. How could she judge Tracey when in her own mind she would've done the same thing?

She must convince the other woman to let them go. Appeal to her nurturing side and stall for time. She prayed Jeff had finally returned and helped Mason.

Emma raised her hands and stepped forward. "Tracey, I understand. A parent would do everything to keep their child safe. What did they have you do?"

"They were aware that I worked for your father-in-law and told me to get on the safe house setup team so they could watch all the witnesses."

"How did you convince Seth to let you on the team?"

"By telling him I'd keep close watch over you. I learned about your diabetes, so I told him you required special attention."

"Wait, how did you find out about my medical condition?"

She tilted her head. "I'm a hacker, remember."

"So you break the law to get the information you need? Seth allows that?"

"Hardly. He doesn't know the extent of my capabilities. I spun the truth to get him to put me on the team and used his love for Sierra against him. It was common knowledge he'd do anything for his granddaughter. I also told him I was willing to work lots of overtime and he needed my expertise to keep you safe."

Tracey spoke the truth. Seth doted on his little Tiddlywinks. "How did you find out about my dad, and did you bug the phone you gave me?"

"No. I hacked into his records and added code to receive notifications if any changes in your family's information popped up. So, when they moved him to palliative care, I received a notification. If it was me, I'd want to be told." She bit her lip. "You may find this hard to believe, but I'm not a monster."

Emma remembered all the special touches Tracey had included for her and Sierra at each home. Buying their favorite snacks, bringing Sierra her puzzles and Emma's medical—

"Wait, did you tamper with my insulin?"

Tracey averted her gaze. "I told them no, but an hour later they sent me a video of Cody with duct tape on his mouth. They were going to hurt him. I had no choice."

Emma clenched her jaw, grinding her teeth. The

muscles in her neck throbbed at the thought of the evil this family had inflicted on Tracey. "That poison made my heart stop."

A tear traced down her cheek. "For that, I will always be sorry."

"Did you also set the explosives that almost killed us and hurt Sierra?" Emma wouldn't be so understanding if Tracey had purposely exposed her daughter to danger.

"No. The insulin was the only tampering I did."

Emma's knees buckled, and she shifted her stance to prevent her legs from folding. *Thank You, God.* "Did you put the hits on the dark web?"

"That was Will Gowland. I took over after they killed him, though."

"What else did they have you do?" Emma wanted to know everything. Plus, the more time she gave Mason to find them, the better. It was the only way to stay alive and protect her daughter.

"I kept them updated on all witnesses' locations. I even hacked into WITSEC to find the US safe houses. My brother is Deputy Darryl Rollins."

"I didn't realize Darryl is your brother." What was Emma missing? Then it dawned on her. "Wait! We found his print on the tracking device. Is he helping you?"

"No, I got the trackers from him. I forgot to wipe one of them down. The one in Jerome."

One of them? "That's how you led the assailants to us, isn't it? The one in Jerome and my necklace."

She fingered the heart pendant around her neck. "We wondered how they found Chuck's place. The B&B was supposed to be off everyone's radar."

But that didn't explain how Tracey had found Jeff's cabin. Had they been following them? She had not seen a tail on their trip here. "How did you find us? We found both trackers."

"There's one more." Tracey pointed to Emma's arm. "It's in your CGM."

"What?" Emma ripped off the device and stomped on it, crushing it completely. Would that stop the Luthers from coming?

"It's too late, Emma. They know you're here."

A wave of dizziness attacked her. She split her stance to remain upright and shut her eyes, praying for the moment to pass. Breathing in and out, she exhaled through her mouth.

"You okay?"

Emma opened her eyes. "What do you think? You're still pointing a gun at me."

Tracey angled the weapon. "I'll put it away if you promise not to try anything."

"I will behave." *Unless I see an opening to overpower you.* "There's still something I don't understand. Lincoln was in prison and is now dead. How could he be doing this from his grave?"

Tracey put the gun away. "Lincoln has nothing to do with this. The only thing he's been guilty of is the smuggling conviction. They framed him for everything else."

Emma's neck muscles locked. "Who's responsible for all this, then?"

The boathouse door burst open, and Layla Luther stood with a rifle aimed in Emma's direction.

Her dark eyes personified the evil her father had displayed. Gone was the good, compassionate image she'd presented on camera.

Tracey stepped backward, clearly letting Layla take over the conversation.

"It's been me all along." Layla moved closer to Emma. "You and your boyfriend had no idea."

She was right. Emma had suspected Lance and perhaps others in Luther Shipping, but Layla had always been kind. What was her endgame?

"Why, Layla? Don't you have a good thing going with Layla's Centre of Hope? You're helping so many women. Why put that in jeopardy?"

Her eyes softened for a split second before turning to ice. "Because he threatened to take away everything I'd built."

"Your father?"

"Yes. That maniac threatened to cut me off if I didn't help build his empire."

Emma put her hands on her hips. "Didn't he have enough money?"

"Someone was embezzling. However, the culprit has been taken care of."

A sudden chill slinked through her body, bringing a gnawing sensation of dread. "What are you talking about?"

"Will Gowland was stealing from the family. I had Nadine kill him."

"So his death wasn't because we caught him in our sting?"

"Hardly. It was just a great opportunity to make it look that way. However, you and your boyfriend have proven to be hard to eliminate." She waved her gun. "So, I'll be doing it myself. You know what they say? When you want something done right, do it yourself." She laughed.

She truly was the corrupt Luther. *God, help me. Keep her talking.*

"Did your father really commit suicide?"

"Are you kidding? With his haughty attitude? I pushed him out the window myself."

Emma's breath caught. The air took on a poisonous atmosphere. If this woman had killed her own father, she would not think twice about eliminating everyone in her way. Even a four-year-old child. *Lord, save my baby girl.*

"How did your father get out of prison? Our evidence was airtight."

"Who do you think gave you all the information to put him away in the first place?" She sneered. "I was the one who sent you the ledgers."

Suddenly, the woman's plan came to light for Emma. "You framed him to get rid of him? But it didn't work, did it?"

"No. He threatened me from prison, telling me he knew what I did and putting a hit out on me. I had to beat him to the punch. That's when I enlisted Darlene's help. To cast suspicion onto her. She thinks I'm her friend. Fooled her, too."

You truly are evil. "And you made it look like the task force bungled the investigation to get him out of prison, so you could kill him?"

Layla waggled her finger. "Good girl. You're smarter than you look."

"What I don't get is the why. Why risk everything?"

"That's easy. I needed money to fund Layla's Centre of Hope. Daddy found out I was struggling and was about to pull all funding."

"He abused you, didn't he?" she asked quietly.

"Takes one to know one. Brady hurt you, right?"

Emma's legs weakened. "How did you learn about that?"

"I spent weeks investigating every person on your task force. I'm aware of everything."

But how would she know when Emma had kept it a secret?

"I can almost hear what you're thinking. Tracey here gave me all your medical records. I saw the multiple visits you made to the hospital after you were first married. Remember, I also made all the same excuses." She touched the scar on her face. "I covered enough bruises in my day to recognize what an abused woman looks like."

"Why did Lance come and see me and Mason? What's his role in all this?"

"My brother is such an idiot. He thought he could persuade you to come to Buffalo as an act of faith. He doesn't know what I've done."

Emma narrowed her eyes at Layla. "But doesn't he get half of the Luther empire?"

"It took some swaying, but I convinced Will to get Dad to take Lance out of the estate. My brother didn't want any part of the business anyway, so why should he get the money? I promised Will a cut, but then I found out the weasel was stealing from Dad. I put the hit out on him and all the witnesses. No one messes with Layla Luther."

Emma suppressed the urge to tackle the woman and sneaked a peek from the corner of her eye to search for a weapon. She had to get her daughter out of here. Before this mad woman acted. She crossed her arms and felt the bulge in her pocket, curbing a gulp. They hadn't removed her gun. The bulky man's coat concealed the weapon.

Now to determine the right moment to pull it out.

"Mommy!" Sierra yelled.

Her daughter's screech caught Layla off guard. "Why, you little brat!" The woman stepped toward Sierra.

Now, Emma.

She glanced at Tracey. "Save my daughter," she whispered. "You can't let Layla hurt her." She eased the gun from her pocket, revealing her intent. "Please. I promise, I will help find Cody. Get Sierra out of here."

"Wait, Layla."

Would the computer tech betray Emma again?

"Let me help. I can quiet her down." Tracey walked over to Sierra. "I'm good with kids."

"Fine," Layla muttered.

Emma stilled until the woman moved back to her original position.

Tracey put her gun away and lifted Sierra into her arms.

It was time.

Emma pointed out the window. "Looks like the police are here to take you down."

Layla turned.

Emma whipped out the gun and lunged for the Luther woman. "Go, Tracey!" She shoved Layla into the wall, holding the Glock to her temple.

Sierra's cries intensified.

"You'll regret this, Tracey. My men will kill your son."

Emma pushed her harder. "You're done."

Tracey bolted out of the boathouse with a screaming Sierra.

Emma glanced to ensure they got away.

But her action was enough to allow Layla to act. She headbutted Emma, causing her to stumble backward.

The crazed woman once again raised her rifle and snatched the Glock from Emma's hand. "No, *you're* done. Time for you to take a little walk off the pier." She pushed her toward the door.

No, not water. Another wave of dizziness plagued Emma. Her worst nightmare was about to come true.

Lord, protect me and help Tracey get Sierra to safety.

Cries from a screeching Sierra brought Mason to a standstill. He listened again to determine the direction of her screams. The rain pounded the area. He wiped the drops from his face and peered into the darkness.

A shadow skulked a few yards ahead of them.

"Over there! Let's approach as quietly as possible. We don't want to spook whoever has Sierra." Mason didn't wait for a reply but stepped toward the four-year-old's wailing racket. *Lord, help us get my niece to safety.*

Pain pierced his arm, and he bit the inside of his mouth to distract himself. He needed to focus on Sierra and Emma. Not himself.

He pressed his weakened legs forward.

The noise intensified. They were close.

Mason raised his weapon and turned the flashlight on at the same time. "Stop. Police."

A woman snapped her gaze toward them. Her hood fell off her head, exposing her face.

"Tracey!" Darryl pushed past him.

"Wait." Mason couldn't let the marshal's interference impede Sierra's safety.

"Tracey, it's me." Darryl raised his weapon.

She stopped. "Thank God you're here. We need to keep Sierra from Layla Luther."

"Layla?" Mason had suspected the wrong Luther. He was convinced Lance was behind everything.

"Y'ncle Mason. Bad woman. Mama!" Sierra's garbled words came in between her cries.

"Tracey, what happened?" Mason asked. "Where's Emma?"

Tears blended with raindrops on the computer technician's face. "I'm so sorry. This is all my fault."

"Trace, I told him they have Cody," Darryl said. "Tell us what happened. How did you get away?"

"Emma created a distraction and told me to run." Tracey wiped the rain from Sierra's face. "I couldn't let anything happen to this sweet girl. I've done too much damage as it is. I just pray I haven't killed my only child in the process."

"Where's Emma?" Mason demanded.

"Still in the boathouse. She lunged for Layla and yelled at me to run. I grabbed Sierra and got out quickly." She paused. "Mason, save her. I heard Layla order her to the pier. She's gonna kill her."

A thunderstorm on the water was not a good combination. Plus, Brady had told him Emma hated water.

Another bolt of lightning lit the sky, followed by an explosive clap of thunder.

Sierra screamed and buried her face in Tracey's chest.

They had to get his niece to safety. "Darryl, take them to the cabin."

The marshal holstered his weapon. "What are you going to do?"

"Save Emma."

The deputy squeezed Mason's shoulder. "Be safe." He shone his flashlight in the opposite direction. "Trace, this way."

Mason waited to ensure the trio retreated to safety, and once the bouncing light faded in the distance, he raced toward the pier.

Angry shouts drew his attention, and he made a beeline toward the commotion, ignoring the rain hammering his already soaked and weary body. Emma's life depended on his protection, and he wouldn't let her down. *Lord, give me strength.*

He reached the pier's edge.

Layla pointed her rifle at Emma, commanding her to walk to the end. Emma tripped but caught herself.

He had to move before Layla pushed her into the water.

Fork lightning flashed.

Crack!

The bolt hit an oak tree, splitting it in two and blocking his path to Emma. The oak's heavy trunk fell onto the pier and severed the structure from the land. The dock floated away from the shore.

No! Tightness gripped his chest as he searched for a way to get to the woman he loved. He'd have to face the obstacle course head-on.

He backed up and bolted, willing strength into his legs. He sprinted over the tree trunk and leaped into the air, landing on the pier's end. His feet dangled in the water and he scrambled onto the dock, pain shooting through his left arm.

Mason righted himself just as Layla turned in his direction.

"Stop." Mason reached for his gun only to find the weapon missing. He must have dropped it in his struggle to get onto the floating dock.

He searched his foggy mind for possible takedown scenarios. Mason stumbled toward the duo.

"Good, you're here." Layla pushed Emma closer to the edge. "You can die with your girlfriend."

"Not if I can help it. Give it up, Layla. Authorities are on the way here as we speak." Mason wished he believed his statement. His father had to fight through all the downed trees in the storm plaguing the area. He took another two steps.

"Hardly. You don't think I came alone, did you?" She snapped her fingers.

Three men emerged from the tree line with their guns aimed at Mason.

"Time to surrender, Constable." Layla poked the rifle into Emma's side. "You have no way out."

"How does Lance feel about all of this?" Mason stalled and prayed for his father's team to reach them.

"He gave up his right to any of our father's legacy years ago when he tried to ruin my reputation. I swore to myself I would make him pay. I made sure dcar old Dad removed him from the will."

"How did you do that?" Mason inched closer.

The click of a weapon loading behind him cemented his limbs. He knew if he took another step, his actions might mean his or Emma's life. Or both.

"Didn't take much, since they fought constantly," Layla said. "Plus, I didn't do it. I sweet-talked Will into tricking him. Worked like a charm."

"She killed Lincoln." Emma squirmed in Layla's hold. "Pushed him from his penthouse."

"So, his death wasn't suicide." Nothing surprised him with the Luther family. Mason guessed they hid many more skeletons in their closets.

"Well, none of you will live to tell my lie." She nudged Emma closer to the edge.

Emma fought to regain her footing. "Sierra?"

Sirens sounded in the distance.

His father was almost here.

"Safe." He raised his hands and took another step. "Layla, where is Cody Smith? Give up the boy."

"He's in a secure location, but Tracey will pay for betraying me." She waved her rifle toward the woods. "They won't get to you in time. My men are highly trained. Your father will not get by my mercenary team. I've paid them well."

"I wouldn't write my father's team off that quickly. They're experienced."

She turned the gun on him. "I'm done with this conversation."

They were out of time. Mason had to go to plan B.

Whatever that was.

"You think killing the chief superintendent's son and daughter-in-law won't raise flags?"

"Not when I make your deaths look like a murder-suicide."

He braced his fists at his sides. "You're crazy. No way my father would believe that."

"You underestimate me." She shoved Emma closer to the end. "Then, I'm going to find your sweet daughter, and—"

"No." Emma screamed like a banshee and shoved Layla. The woman's rifle clattered to the dock.

The Luther daughter stumbled into Mason, shoving them both off the pier.

His head hit a steel buoy just as he plunged into the water, sinking into murky darkness.

"What have I done?" Emma had saved herself but sacrificed the man she loved. "God, please save him. I want him in my life."

Emma scanned the water for Mason. No signs of him surfaced.

Gunfire erupted from the shoreline. Bullets splintered the deck at her feet. Emma dived to the wooden surface to shield herself from the danger.

The rain had stopped hammering the area, but her earlier ominous feelings remained.

Layla's men dashed to the lake's edge.

Emma's heartbeat thrashed in her ears. She covered her head to block the noise.

Angry shouts caught her attention. She peeked at the shore.

Seth's men emerged from the trees.

"Police. Stop," Seth yelled. "You're surrounded."

Multiple shots rang out.

The constables returned fire. Men dropped.

Layla burst out of the lake, clutching the pier's side.

Emma eyed the discarded rifle a few feet away. It was imperative she reach the weapon before Layla did. Emma scurried to her feet and leaped forward, but was too late.

Layla had scrambled onto the deck and reached the rifle first. She snatched the weapon and stood. "You're going to pay for that. You killed your boyfriend, and now I'm going to kill you. Then your daughter."

"No!" Emma's jellylike legs prevented movement. She took a breath and mustered courage, willing her limbs to work as she faced the evil

Layla Luther head-on. "You will not get away with all the killing you've done."

"Who's stopping me?"

Emma pointed to the shore. "They are."

Layla turned.

Seth and his team had apprehended Layla's henchmen, and Seth had his rifle trained on Layla. "Drop your weapon, Miss Luther. You have no-where to go, and your men are all in custody."

"You'll never take me alive. If I die, she dies."

The clouds broke, and the moon illuminated the area. Emma once again scanned the lake, search-ing for Mason. *Lord, help me find him.*

Seconds later, she spotted him under a stretch of water where the moon beamed. He had surfaced and was gulping air, his arms flailing. He was con-scious but obviously in trouble.

Emma turned to the men at the shoreline. They were too far away. No way could they get to Mason in time. She was his only hope. The hair at the nape of her neck prickled. She hated the water, but she loved the man.

"Your time is up," Layla said. She raised the rifle.

A shot rang out, and Layla dropped to the deck.

Seth's aim met its target.

Emma glanced back at Mason. His body stilled. She needed to act now if he had any hope of sur-vival. She ignored her fears, summoned courage and dived into the water. Despite the warm air, the cool lake chilled her to the bones. She surfaced, gulped in air, relocated Mason and swam toward him, kicking hard and fast.

Emma reached him quickly. She turned him over and clasped her hold under his arms.

"Hurry, Emma. Save my boy." Seth's frantic voice boomed from the small beach.

She gathered strength and tugged Mason toward the water's edge. Emma kicked harder, her adrenaline spiking. Within minutes, she reached the shore.

Seth bolted to meet them and helped her bring him to the riverbank. He shone a light on his son's ashen face. His previous bump had swelled to a goose egg on Mason's forehead.

Emma placed her fingers on his neck. His pulse was weak. She leaned close to his mouth. "He's not breathing." She began CPR. "Come on, Mason." Tears cascaded down her wet cheeks. "Don't leave me, too."

Seconds later, he coughed, and water spewed from his mouth.

She turned him on his side to allow any excess to drain away. "You're okay. I've got you."

Mason grabbed her arm. "Layla?"

Seth knelt beside them. "She's dead. Her men are in custody. It's over, son. You're all safe."

"Thank You, God." Mason rubbed his head.

"Paramedics are en route. They'll check you all out, including Sierra." The man's voice hitched, and he paused, glancing at each of them. "I'm so proud of both of you. You're stronger together. Don't let that go to waste."

Emma caught Mason's gaze and held.

Seth was right. They *were* stronger together.

Her father-in-law cleared his throat. "I'll give you some privacy." He walked to his team.

"Help me sit." Mason's raspy words could barely be heard over the waves slapping the shoreline.

Emma placed her hand under his right arm and brought him to a seated position. She grazed the bump on his head. "You okay?"

Mason cupped his hand over hers. "Don't worry about me. Did Layla hurt you?"

She shook her head.

"Listen, I'm sorry for getting angry at you earlier." He paused. "Deep down, I realized you were telling me the truth about Brady. I just didn't want to admit the brother I idolized would hurt you."

"Yes, it's hard to believe."

"I want you to know something. I would never do that. You're an incredible woman and one who deserves to be treated with love and respect."

Even though the man before her looked and sounded like her late husband, Emma recognized Mason spoke the truth. She'd witnessed his gentle mannerisms with her and Sierra throughout the past week.

She pulled her hand away and caressed his face. "And I want you to know… I'm not Zoe. I would never betray an amazing man like you. Observing you throughout the years has proved to me you're not like Brady. It just took me till now to admit your gentleness to myself."

Her feelings finally dawned on Emma. It was time. Time to open her heart to the man who'd stolen her every waking thought and her daughter's love.

Time to put the life with Brady behind her. But would Mason accept her love?

God had proved that even though her life's journey held many twists and turns, one thing remained consistent. He had been right beside her the entire time. It was time to trust in Him, even if it meant Mason wasn't ready.

She inched closer to him, eyeing his lips. "Mason, I need to tell you something." She inhaled. "I want you—"

His lips smothered her in a tender kiss, interrupting her words and stealing her breath.

But in a good way.

Emma hated to end the moment, but she finally pulled back. "I love you, Mason James."

He moved a curl from her face, his fingers lingering. "And I love you, Emma James."

Thank You, God. He'd not only given her renewed life in Him, but the man of her dreams to share it with.

Forever.

EPILOGUE

Eighteen months later

Mason lifted Sierra into his arms, grabbed his wife's hand and walked down the courthouse steps. Today all his heart's desires had come true. He'd not only married the woman of his dreams, but the court had just granted his request. Sierra's adoption had finally been approved. Sierra James was now officially his daughter.

Daughter.

The word brought him uncontainable joy.

The little girl cuddled his face. "Papa!"

His heart hitched, and he turned his gaze to the beautiful redhead beside him. "I'm bursting inside."

Emma leaned closer and kissed his cheek. "Me, too, my love. We're now officially a family."

Mason could not believe the blessings God had bestowed on him after such a dramatic week eighteen months ago. A week that would forever be etched in his mind. A week that had changed his life.

Chief Superintendent Seth James had taken the news of his beloved Brady's abuse hard, but eventually he'd confessed he suspected something was off with his son. He just hadn't wanted to face the fact it could have been true. He also apologized to Mason for his years of not believing in his son.

Father and son begged each other for forgiveness, and they'd embraced in a hug Mason would remember forever. They had both sobbed, washing away years of pain from losing a wife, mother, son and brother. Their strained relationship instantly bonded into a strong one and still stood true today.

The chief superintendent announced his retirement and promoted his son—all in one week. Seth James commended Mason in a press conference for his hard work in bringing the Luther family to justice. They released all witnesses from the protection program.

Lance Luther took his sister's death and betrayal hard. Even though they hadn't been close, he mourned her loss. He proved to be the more compassionate Luther when he took over his sister's nonprofit organization, Layla's Centre of Hope. Lance told the public his sister had still done so much good for abused women, and he wanted to turn that part of her legacy into a blessing. For the wickedness she had imposed, he reached out to all the families of the loved ones she had killed and left them a sizable amount of cash. He also publicly praised US and Canadian authorities for all their hard work in protecting the other witnesses, sincerely apologizing for his sister's actions.

Authorities incarcerated Tracey Smith for her

part in Layla's scheme—even though she'd done it under duress. Emma's testimony to Tracey's character would go a long way in getting the woman an early parole.

Emma had mourned her father's death with Daphne and Holly Williams. She confessed saying goodbye to her father was the hardest thing she'd ever had to do, but praised God they'd see her father again one day. It was a hope every Christian held in their hearts.

After healing from his wounds, Mason and Emma had dated for two months before he popped the question. He had already wasted too much time in his life and vowed he'd not let more days go by without Emma. They married six months later.

Today, his daughter's adoption sealed his family.

Sierra tugged on Mason's collar. "Papa. Let's celebrate."

The little girl's vocabulary had sprouted over the last few months.

Mason kissed Sierra's cheek. "Where would you like to go, my sweet daughter?"

"McDonald's!"

A five-year-old's idea of fancy dining.

Mason glanced at his wife. "Well?"

Emma shrugged. "Fine by me." She rubbed her tummy. "I have a sudden craving for fish."

Mason stopped. "What are you saying, Em?"

She grinned. "You're gonna be a father. *Again.*"

"What?" He pulled her closer and kissed her lips. "God is good."

"All the time." Emma squeezed Sierra's nose. "Did you hear that, baby girl? You're gonna have a little brother or sister."

Sierra clapped. "Yay! Supper first?"

Mason tousled his daughter's curls. "Yes, Sisi, supper first."

Once again, he grabbed his wife's hand and squeezed. A tear slipped down his cheek, and he marveled at the goodness God had given him.

Not only had the Lord proven His love for Mason by wrapping His protective arms around him, but He also gave him everything Mason could have ever desired.

A wife, family and eternal love.

* * * * *

*If you liked this story from Darlene L. Turner,
check out her previous
Love Inspired Suspense books:*

Border Breach
Abducted in Alaska
Lethal Cover-Up

Available now from Love Inspired Suspense!

*Find more great reads at
www.LoveInspired.com.*

Dear Reader,

I hope you enjoyed reading Mason, Emma and Sierra's story as much as I loved crafting their adventure. It was fun to include a four-year-old in the mix and watch how she responds to danger. These characters will be challenged while constantly running from each threat.

Mason and Emma both feel God blindsided them with their struggles. They had their lives all planned out, but their paths changed, and in their eyes, not for the good. However, they will eventually see God's timing is perfect and He knows best. This is something we all battle with at times, right? Trust even in the midst of trials. God is our protector through everything.

I'd love to hear from you. You can contact me through my website, www.darlenelturner.com, and also sign up for my newsletter to receive exclusive subscriber giveaways. Thanks for reading my story.

God bless,
Darlene L. Turner

Get 4 FREE REWARDS!

We'll send you 2 FREE Books plus 2 FREE Mystery Gifts.

Harlequin Heartwarming Larger-Print books will connect you to uplifting stories where the bonds of friendship, family and community unite.

FREE Value Over **$20**